...REVOLTING TALES...

Christopher D. Abbott
Todd A. Curry

ISBN: 149288474X
ISBN-13: 978-1492884743

Dedication

I would like to thank the following people in no particular order.

My dearly departed parents. Where in a moment in time and a twinkle in one's eye created me. And to all nine of my brothers, Sparky, Garry, Jody, George, Mickey Randy, Cleon, Tommy, and Fred, who provided years of loving humiliation that helped transform me into the man I am today.

And expressly to my dearest wife and closest friend. A true soul mate to whom at the end of each day I can contribute our fractional ups and downs to her untiring understanding of me and all that drives me.

And last but not least, to my co-author Chris, a little man with a big imagination and amazing literary talent.

TAC

I dedicate this book to Carol *"Dinger"* Mancini. Who has continually supported me, been a friend, a mom, a champion. Bless you.

Huge thanks to the following people: Richard Sutton, Mike Valentino, Todd, Alison, Trayc, and Mum and Dad.

CDA

Table of Contents

INTRODUCTION

By Christopher D. Abbott

The following stories you're about to read are, well, pretty awful. Todd and I both use the term: for the rude, crude, and abusive – and that's very accurate. When I embarked on this project with Todd, I didn't have any expectations of where it would go, or how we would get there. Todd had the ideas, and I had the ability to take those ideas and develop them. Initially we set out to simply write some twisted stories, they had nothing in common with each other, they were just fun to write. We would sit and discuss them, create disgustingly grotesque situations and put nasty vile people into them and it worked well. Until, that is, we created the characters of Lou and Sandra – that's when things started to change.

Anyone who knows Todd well will certainly recognise that the character of Lou is based on him, and sadly it follows that the character of Sandra is based on me....

So then the stories you're about to read are still pretty awful, crude, vile, and yes juvenile at times, and – well – cringingly gross, there is a method to them. A thread runs through them all, a theme, if you like, and we hope you enjoy them for what they are: harmlessly grotesque, disgustingly inspired, horrifyingly funny, and above all, we sincerely hope, entertaining.

By Todd A. Curry

Guess what I've got in my hand, and I'll give you a bite.

Many people over the years have encouraged me to write a book, and despite several attempts to do so, I often fell back on my gene-pool roots and moved onto something else. You see I am "that guy". You can simply describe me with a single cliché: *I am a jack of all trades, master of none.* I come from a gene-pool that gave me the blueprint and the ability to be someone great, conversely, somewhere in that same gene-pool, I was forced to take the path of least resistance, to simply do only what was necessary to get by.

I had attempted, many times, to put in writing my thoughts and stories, but discovered I often lacked sequence and details. My writing never quite depicted enough detail in order to grab the reader's attention, until I met Chris, a unique little character, from a completely different demographic and social background. He is truly the Abbot to Costello and even more comparably, Felix to Oscar, from *The Odd Couple*. I'm sure you can guess where I fall into that comparison. We discovered we had a common passion for music. I had not played the saxophone for 30 years and, like a true jack of all trades, never played it very well. After my retirement, I was looking for the right reasons to pick it up again. I found that reason after discovering Chris was an extremely talented musician. We developed a close friendship - just a "bromance" people, strictly platonic – and I subsequently found the courage I needed to show him some of my writing. He appeared intrigued and agreed to write my autobiography. Chris dug deep enough into my life, with my autobiography, and a trust was formed. I was comfortable telling him things I thought I would never repeat. He appeared impressed with my off the wall way of interpreting everyday life. I explained writing was a release for me in order to keep my sanity. My off the wall thoughts and odd way of looking at things, and Chris' uncanny ability to take those ideas and develop them, quickly turned into collaboration. My attempts to simply get by were often thwarted during my thirty some odd years as a cop, both in the military, and civilian world, by scenarios so serious, it was impossible to remain invisible, and or insignificant. Luckily the end result happened in my favour. I'm still here. These scenarios made great story telling for me and many found them both entertaining and enlightening. I have friends and family who have looked forward to another story, embellished and at times fabricated in order to make it worth telling, or to keep the listener's attention.

These stories may well be considered crude or simply considered awful, by many, but are in no way meant to offend. I also know there are many of you out there who aren't willing to admit you have a twisted side. So these stories are written to entertain. To remind you we all have inner demons of our own and left unchecked I fear they may consume me, so I unleash them, to consume you instead...

...you were warned...

ౠఆ

...there's no turning back now...

Lou...

In his infinitesimal yet grotesquely cosy office far beneath the world, basking in the devilish delights of his unique domain sat the most powerful being in the underworld. He had many names, various guises, and billions of living, and the not so living, creatures across millions of worlds knew him, feared him, and all with good reason. At this moment in his timeless existence he was simply known as Lou.

A pair of gold rimmed half-moon spectacles perched on the end of a high nose, which led to a haughty-brow. Large lidless eyes, a kaleidoscope of yellows and reds continually changing, sparkling, burning, darted left and right as he read through the latest book that Sandra had written for him.

Sandra.

His loyal enigma.

She was as much a part of him, as he was of her. They existed physically separate, each a façade, different, yet the same.

Throughout the eons they existed as one.

Lou, the tormentor.

Sandra, the organiser.

The room was meticulously adorned with memorabilia from every culture on every world. Some of the most disgusting, depraved and generally tasteless forms of art that anyone outside of Lou's closest friends (not that he had friends as we understand the term) was ever likely to see, hung around the room in spotless glass cases, or mounted on wooden plinths. The uniqueness of his collection could not be matched. All of his prized possessions were corporeal, but not in the same way as the "living". Existing in the underworld or Hell was analogous to "living", except certain rules that applied to one, were not applicable to the other. It didn't matter the type of person or species, the convergent nature of Hell was symbiotic with that person's understanding of existence. That the horrendous mutilations or representations of one form or another were part of their own perceived concept of what Hell should be like, because their original consciousness was still intact, added credence to this symbiosis. The gruesome nature of the punishments, the dismemberment, the displacement of mind, body, and soul, or other incalculably terrifying and surreal cruelties imposed on the victims of Hell, actually came from the minds of those who received it – that was the incongruity of it. It was ephemeral pleasure for Lou, everlasting torment for the victim.

Like the old song says: *You can checkout anytime you like, but you can never leave.*

Lou prided himself on his creativity. Above his desk hung a light in the shape of a bug zapper; its ultraviolet bulbs glowed blue-purple, and welded to the outside of the cage, a miniature half man half dragonfly, continuously twitching and bucking, voiceless, his tiny human face contorted in eternal suffering. The fire burned his body but it didn't consume him. It illuminated just enough light for Lou to read. Occasionally he chuckled. He flicked over a page and picked up the glass to his right. He noted with mild annoyance its emptiness. He placed it down on the table, reached over to the intercom buzzer and pressed a button firmly down.

'Sandra?'

There was a brief pause and a voice reverberated through a crackly speaker.

'Lou?'

'Sandra, my drink is empty.'

'Really?' The scorn in her voice poured through the intercom like sour milk.

'Yes, really. Can you make me another? I mean, if it's not too much of an inconvenience.'

He heard her sigh.

'Okay, but just so you know, I'm running very low on Nigerian cocks.'

Lou snorted.

'What about Libyan?'

'Fine, just… I just want a drink. Is that too much to ask?'

He reached over and pressed the off button. With a dramatic sigh, he continued to read. Ten minutes later, Sandra shuffled in. She was a petit older woman who dressed as if she was twenty years younger. Her greying hair pulled tight, wound into a bun, an array of pencils holding it firmly in place. She carried a tray with two full cocktail glasses of vomit-like liquid. Lou looked up and gave a gratifying smile. He couldn't be annoyed with her for long. She smirked as she placed the tray down on the table opposite the archaic black and white television. He stood and removed his glasses, placing them neatly in a case. He closed it and straightened out his jacket.

Blowing out the flame on the burning dragonfly-man he finally sat. Sandra handed him a glass, took her own, and snuggled up beside him.

He sipped the contents and sighed happily.

'Ah… that's amazing. Do I detect a hint of Catholic priest spleen?'

She nodded politely. 'It adds a certain flare, a little bite, don't you think?'

Lou savoured another sip and said, 'So where are we with my itinerary for the week?'

Sandra carefully placed her glass on the table between them, pulled a notebook out of thin air and flipped to an empty page.

'Well, let me see. You have that appointment with Joseph at ten today, then there's that business with the third level we still have to fix.'

Lou grimaced. 'That's still a problem?'

'Apparently they are talking about starting a union.'

'Are you being serious?

'Perfectly, I assure you.'

'Don't they know this is Hell?'

'Apparently that message appears to have been lost.'

'Flush the worst down a level. Who have we got down there, anyway?'

'Vladimir?'

'The Impaler?'

She nodded.

'Oh perfect. I loved the way he roasted children and fed them to their mothers. He is a real connoisseur. I remember the first time we met, it was just after he'd cut off the breasts of a group of women and forced their husbands to eat them. After that, he had them all impaled… yes, send them there.'

'And the others?'

'I don't know, Sandra, you think of something. Something.... Nasty. No, wait, something really nasty.'

'*Really* nasty?' She raised an eyebrow. 'Like Hell isn't *really* nasty enough, nasty?'

'Apparently it's not,' Lou said shaking his head. 'Unions....'

'Well,' she said and paused to consider. 'I was floating that idea about the pinworm epidemic. I could have them all transformed to eggs and infect someone – but keep them conscious. How's that?'

'Tame.'

Sandra flicked through her notepad. Lou looked off into the distance. Then a sudden thought occurred, causing a growing smile to spread across his devilish face.

'Open up the conference hall, that really large *echoy* one, and lock them all in.'

Her smile spread too. 'Liberace?'

'Liberace,' he crooned. 'Hours, no weeks, no years of Liberace.'

Sandra flicked the pad one more time.

'You have a busy few days do you want me to put off your weekly with Gabe?'

Lou shook his head. 'I'd love to, but I'd better not.'

'There are about ninety-thousand new arrivals today from Earth, of those about twenty-thousand are "specials".'

Lou rubbed his goatee and beamed. *Specials: people who required my specific attention. The people who led the kind of life granting them an express pass to the lowest levels of Hell.*

Lou put his drink down beside Sandra's.

'Let's see what's on the box, shall we?' He made a "clap-clap" with his hands and the television flicked on. It brightened slowly and a snowy-static-filled picture emerged on the screen. He stretched out, crossed his cloven feet, and picked up his glass cradling it in both hands. Sandra plumped up a pillow and put it behind her. Eventually the screen cleared....

The screen displays a classic 1960s horror typographic entitled:

"Revolting Tales: Episode One"

It is night. A camera follows a car as it speeds down a wide dusty track towards a derelict old mansion. Two teenagers are in the front; the one driving takes a swig from a bottle of Jack Daniels and hands it to the passenger. He too takes a gulp and leans across the dashboard, pointing.

'Go down there!'
The camera zooms out and up, showing us the view from atop an old house. A gargoyle statue glints in the moonlight. We see the car entering a huge overgrown circular driveway. In its centre, on what appears to be a heavily overgrown lawn sits a massive willow tree. The car stops in the driveway.

They exit the vehicle. The passenger runs to the tree. 'I gotta piss.'

The driver now sits in the passage seat, he shouts out to his friend, who finishes and runs to take the wheel. The car speeds off and back down the lane. The camera stays in the same position, but slowly zooms in on the tree. Off screen we hear the noise of the car as it makes its way back, the tree now almost fills the screen.

There is the sound of tires screeching followed by a violent crash. The camera slowly pans towards the car, the front of which is embedded into the tree. The car backs up and then speeds away, the passenger is screaming and cursing. As the car disappears out of shot, the camera pans back to the tree. Standing next to it is a little girl in a dirty off-white nightdress with shoulder length black hair. She pets the tree for a moment, and then she looks back at the camera.

Her expressionless face changes to a snarl as she lets out a long, angry scream…

Episode One:

Escaping Matilda

'No, no, no! Stay and play with me.' The voice was close to a whisper, just enough to hear, but with impenetrable darkness around him, Billy Mason couldn't discern the owner – although he had a pretty good idea.

He'd pushed himself away from the voice, hobbling towards the only visible thing in the room; a door. He listened for some time but there were no sounds coming from outside. His heart pounded. It beat so hard it hurt. He didn't really understand where he was, or how he'd got there. All he knew was he was trapped inside a house – an empty old house.

A soft giggle to his right made him cry in terror.

The room was too dark to see anything clearly, except the doorway. Billy didn't think too hard about it, didn't fully appreciate that the light was unnatural. Renewed adrenaline charged through him, as he yanked open the door and, without pause, ran headlong into the hallway to sprint towards the house's entrance. He fell as the pain from his broken ankle coursed through him, but the same adrenaline that gave him the strength to push on, picked him up, and he continued to stagger through the empty hallway. He'd been afraid Matilda might be waiting for him. Standing there with that nasty looking mutilated rabbit she carried. He saw her in his minds-eye, her black eyes unblinking, her equally black hair dancing across her filthy white nightgown. His intention was to just run at her, to knock the little shit down, to stampede her and then he could escape through the doorway into the night beyond.

But she wasn't there. The hallway was empty, the front door shut.

Again the only visible light was directed at the door. Billy barged into it, so desperate in his desire to escape, his shoulder took the impact. He fumbled for the latch, twisted it, and pulled the door towards him. His fingers slipped from the metal, as the door remained firmly shut. He tried again, this time using both hands, twisting and pulling. The latch grew brittle and became a raised surface of sharp metal fragments that cut his fingers to shreds. He continued with all his strength to pull at it, and despite the fact blood now flowed freely from his wounds he did not give in. His muscles ached as he tried in vain to wrench the damn thing open. As if to add additional strength, he screamed at it. Again, nothing happened, the door refused to budge. His fingers were now a pulped bloody mess and almost useless. The pain eventually forced him to stop. In desperation he pushed a thin arm through the letterbox to try and get to the latch on the other side. Hysterical now, tears flowing, ignoring the pain of his arm, blood seeping back through the letterbox as he twisted and inched as hard as he could until he found the latch. Elbow deep, Billy's concentration was exact. The sense of relief was euphoric, but that too was muted by the fact that no matter how hard he tried, the door simply *would not open*. His entire arm and shoulder were numb with the spent energy - with the force he used - and eventually the revelation finally dawned on him. He wasn't escaping through the front door.

It hit him like a duelling man's open hand slap to the face.

He staggered back, cradling his ripped and bruised arm. His fear response was so extreme he couldn't even form coherent words as he cursed it, screamed at it. And Billy understood now. Like the house and everything in it, the door had a will of its own and it didn't *want* to open.

Billy blindly hobbled to the back of the house, down twisting corridors that defied logic.

How big was this house anyway?

Again he fell from a misstep on his broken ankle. The last corridor he found led to what appeared to be a large kitchen and that was when he remembered seeing a broken window in the pantry. That was his only chance, he knew it. He limped as fast as he could, using the only good arm he had left to brace against the wall, taking the weight off his mangled foot, he ran straight into a beam of light.

And then he stopped dead. Something felt wrong, terribly wrong.

Billy stood and watched in horror as around him lights appeared in circles on the floor. Wisps of smoky vapours curled in grotesque approximations of snakes, up and into the room, and unspeakable things manifested and gathered around him, their misty states finally solidifying into unnatural shapes, preening in the colourless light. It was as if they had been waiting for him, knowing he would come.

Sure that he couldn't possibly escape. And as Billy looked up at the pantry window, he saw with a heavy heart, that is wasn't broken at all.

Silhouettes moved in around the glare from the window's light, the worst of their deformities hidden from him. In the aberration of light, Billy caught glimpses of perverted creatures. He saw partial disfigurements that were hellish. Twisted anomalous bodies, mutated and asymmetrical, beyond anything real, yet appearing blissful in their own monstrousness. They revelled in themselves and each other, fondling and caressing, performing lascivious acts on one another, the salaciousness of their pairing, the lustful way they blended was the very juxtaposition of sexual desire and vulgar deviant nightmare.

Billy wasn't able to give the forms names, nor did he recognise what they were, but their couplings were like those of beasts and demons from fables of old. The very air filled with the sounds of unrepressed sexual desire, energy, tension, release, and Billy just stood there, scared beyond belief.

Partially solid hands lightly touched him, their caress producing a sexual energy that transcended anything Billy had ever experienced. They reached up and tore at his shirt. Frozen in fear, he was powerless to act. Light touches against his neck and ears and made his knees tremble. He was conscious of a weight pulling the fly-button open on his Levis exposing his Calvins, aware of ethereal hands reaching inside to feel his flesh, corrupting him with their caress. He fell back against the wall, horrified then appalled, as his own body began responding to their touches, his senses aroused by the pawing, touching, caressing, bringing him to the very brink of both pleasure, and pain. They engulfed him in their wantonness and he was stripped bare by them, physically and emotionally. Pleasure and pain muddled as clothes along with skin, fell with a sickening thud to the floor…

…and Billy screamed so hard, he woke himself up.

Billy sat up in bed and tried to untangle himself from his sweat soaked sheet. He pulled at it but it was wrapped tightly around the orthopaedic boot, it made it difficult to straighten out. He looked up as the door to his room abruptly opened. Standing there, dishevelled and concerned, was his mother. She saw his aroused nakedness and quickly turned away, cursing herself.

'Mom!' Embarrassed, he hastily covered up.

'Sorry, she muttered, her back still turned.

'Jesus Christ.' He rubbed at his face and pulled his phone off the nightstand.

'You decent?'

'Yeah.' He checked the time. 05:00.

'Another nightmare?' she asked as she cautiously entered the room.

He fell back against the pillow and covered his face. 'Uhuh.'

She sat on the edge of his bed carefully. 'Worse than the last?'

He shook his head. 'Not worse, just different. Surreal, I don't know. Bad.'

'Sexy?' she asked trying to break the tension.

'Cute, Ma, real cute.'

'Sorry.'

He rubbed at his sleep deprived eyes. His mother's look of concern bothered him and he managed to smile weakly.

'Billy,' she said pausing to gain his full attention. 'D'you think it might be time to, um, see someone?'

'A shrink?' He gave her a look.

She sighed. 'You've been having these dreams for weeks, ever since you hurted your foot.'

He winced. Inwardly he said, *Hurt, Ma. Not hurted.*

'I know, Ma.' Again he covered his face and groaned.

'I know this guy,' she said as she waited till Billy was looking at her. 'He's discreet, you know? And you won't have to tell him nothing you don't want to.'

Billy groaned again. 'Whatever, Ma.'

She smiled. 'Worse thing you can get is a prescription for something to help you sleep, right?'

'Right,' he said dripping with sarcasm. 'Cos sleeping is a boat load of fun.'

'Good.' She got up. 'He'll set you right, he's a real good guy.'

Something to help me sleep, he thought, *that really was the worst thing I could get right now.*

The room was full of people in various stages of physical and emotional distress. Billy and his mother sat quietly in a set of plastic formed seats waiting to be called. He shifted uncomfortably. *Whoever designed these "butt marks" on the seat must have been really tiny.*

His mother flicked through a year old Cosmopolitan magazine, the headline of which read: "Seventy-Five sex moves to drive him crazy". He looked up at the television, the sound was off, but the news story being retold repetitively by various different news-anchors was the same as it was the previous day: Syria. The whole of the civilised world was up in arms about the use of chemical weapons against a frightened and demoralised people, two million refugees. Thousands dead. Tit-for-tat accusations of who was responsible. Billy sighed, wishing someone would turn the damn thing off. As he focused in on the same twenty-second clip he'd seen five or six times already, the picture turned fuzzy. Static buzzed over the screen and when it cleared, the picture had changed from colour to black and white.

A bead of sweat dripped off his brow. On the screen was a grainy looking picture of a house. An empty house. His heart rate sped up as the camera zoomed slowly towards the front door. Flies buzzed around the screen and then there were flies around Billy. He swatted at them cursing. His mother flicked another page nosily.

Billy eyed movement under the chair ahead of him. Something was moving slowly towards him. He craned his neck and was shocked to see a pool of yellow liquid expanding underneath the chair. The air smelled of urine. He held a hand to his nose and turned to his mother.

'You see that?'

Engrossed in her magazine, as if he wasn't there, she flicked another page. He rolled his eyes and stood up.

'I'm going to the restroom.' He hobbled away without waiting for a response.

Billy entered the bathroom just as an elderly man was leaving. His flamboyant pink shirt was tucked neatly into bright turquoise trousers, heavily stained around the crotch. Noticing his strapped up left foot, the old man carefully held the door open for him. Billy thanked him as he walked past. The elderly man put a nicotine-stained hand on his shoulder, his fingernails ragged and dirty, the skin mottled with liver-spots. He had a pungent odour, like a combination of brie cheese and bleach. He felt the dampness of the fingers on his shirt as they lightly caressed him.

'Want me to hold it for you?' Billy pulled away shocked and the old man continued to watch him. He slowly raised his hands to his face, and sniffed gently at his fingers. Billy hobbled to the urinal and slipped in a puddle of urine. He managed to right himself before he fell, but had to grab the porcelain pisser to do it. The old man hummed slightly, he blinked his watery eyes as he sniffed at his fingers again. Without taking his eyes off Billy, he gently began sucking on them, running his tongue along each finger, pushing them in and out in a lewd, indecent, libidinous fashion. Eventually he turned away, the door closed behind him, leaving Billy alone.

'What the fuck!' Billy cursed and made his way to the sink. He turned on the tap to wash his hands and the water spluttered violently. His face was covered, along with his shirt. His eyes stung and he instinctively rubbed them. His nose picked up the scent before his eyes saw it, the sour coppery stink of blood and gore. He looked at his hands and let out a cry of horror. Blood was everywhere, along the walls, on the floor and overflowing from the sink. It wasn't typical bright-red frothy flowing blood; it was thickly viscous, coagulated, and dark maroon and it moved slowly, like melting wax.

Billy fumbled with the tap until it stopped, and all that could be heard was a dripping sound, as the last few drops fell into the basin.

He looked into the mirror but was unable to see anything, as blood and moisture rendered it useless. He looked around for something he could use to wipe it. Delving into the overflowing garbage can he pulled out a number of damp paper-towels. When the mirror was cleared, his heart missed a beat. What he saw reflected, froze him in fear. It was a girl in a nightdress. She was sitting on the floor with her back to him, vigorously shaking her arms in front of her, but he couldn't see what she was doing. But at this point, it really didn't matter. If she was here, then he must be back in that empty house – but that wasn't possible – unless he was dreaming again.

He dropped the paper-towels.

Time froze.

The dripping from the faucet had almost stopped entirely. Yet somehow, despite his terror, despite the overwhelming dread that threatened to consume him, he turned slowly towards her. Hoping beyond all fathomable reason, it was simply a hallucination, that his mind was playing tricks on him; but it wasn't.

Wide-eyed his terror consumed him and as his bladder emptied itself involuntarily, he entered the first stages of shock, where the mind is numbed and the senses insensible. It *was* Matilda; he knew it. And she turned her head to look at him, a sad expression played across her pallid corpse-like face, her mouth turned downwards, her bottom lip thrust out. She stood, and held in both hands were two parts of the same doll. Except it wasn't a doll. Billy could only watch in abstract horror as blood soaked hands tried again to push the two halves back together. Tiny intestines - snake-like - dangled from the half she held in her right hand.

'I broke it,' she crooned with a childish sulk.

Then angrily she shouted, 'Stupid thing!'

With the tantrum befitting her age in life, she threw both parts of the dead infant at him. They hit the walls with a squelching thud and slid to rest either side of him. He looked down to see the milky glazed eyes. No bigger than a dime.

Billy trembled uncontrollably as Matilda skipped forwards, coming to a stop four feet away from him. Her arms crossed, her toes on each foot flexing back and forth.

'Play with me.' She pouted.

Billy backed away.

Matilda moved closer.

'PLAY WITH ME!'

He felt the world shaking, like an earthquake. He wasn't sure what was happening, and then he heard a familiar voice. His mother's voice.

'Billy!'

His eyes snapped open. His mother stopped vigorously shaking him. Beside her were two nurses and a well-dressed man in a suit. He blinked a few times, his breathing ragged. He was covered in sweat and a nurse was taking his pulse. He looked down at the towel, strategically placed over his crotch. His eyes began to water as he witnessed the look of relief wash over his mother's face.

Billy Mason began to cry, hysterically.

The screen displays a classic 1960s horror typographic entitled:

"Revolting Tales: Episode Two"

A camera slowly pans towards a large house. The lawn is meticulously kept and a pool sits to one side, the water green with algae and dirt. The camera steadily zooms in towards a window. As the camera passes through into the room, we hear the sound of rough sex. A man is grunting and his cadence is broken by a woman's voice.
'Yeah... fuck me!'

Episode Two:

The Gamble

'Can't you just shut-the-fuck up…you nasty twat!'

Why do all women feel they need to talk while I'm fucking them! Marco thought while he fought to maintain his libido. He reached down and grabbed a fist full of hair from the back of her head and squeezed it tightly.

She briefly gasped and then went silent - as he'd demanded.

'I'm not paying you to talk, whore.'

He thrust aggressively, tugging back her head with her hair.

'Lift that ass up higher,' he commanded, gritting his teeth.

Her whole body stiffened with the sudden combination of pain he was inflicting. She complied as best as she could from the doggy style position.

Marco slapped her several times. Not in a kinky erotic way, but more like the way an angry raging mother would strike her obnoxious out of control five-year old.

Each slap was harder than the last. The fifth and final was up alongside her head. That opened hand blow caused her to wince and scream.

And her reaction instantly gratified Marco.

He then let go of her hair and anchored himself, grabbing lose ageing skin from each of her hips. He quickly changed his rhythmic thrusting from slow and forceful, to jack rabbit fast, deep and painful.

She buried her face into the pillow to muffle her painful moans and cries. The lubrication was wearing off as she felt the friction burns. She was hoping he would just finish so she could be on her way with the fifty bucks she was still tightly clutching in her left hand. *She had been warned by the other girls about this guy and how he would short-change her the first chance he got.*

Marco stopped for a brief moment. A look of surprise and curiosity came over him as he reached down with a forefinger and thumb and picked off a small piece of toilet paper stuck to a portion of the hooker's ass. He brought it closer to his eyes in order to focus on it for confirmation.

'Jesus Christ! Don't you fuckin wash your asshole, you nasty pig?'

He quickly rolled it into a ball and flicked it at the back of her head. It stuck to her hair as he started with another volley of deep angry jack rabbit thrusts. With each he winced with an expression as if he was scraping a three-day old road kill off a hot Texas road.

It's amazing what you won't touch with your fingers….but you'll stick your dick in!

Marco felt the beginning of an orgasm. Desperate not to lose it, he gave three or four sharp pumps and with a guttural grunt of pleasure, he collapsed on top of her for a brief moment, and then pushed her away.

'Now get out! And don't steal anything on the way either. I swear, I will hunt you down and crucify your ass.'

Marco rolled off the bed and stood up. He took her underwear and cleaned himself. He then tossed them at her. She caught them and hissed angrily. She stood up and quickly put on her tight fitting hip hugging dress, grabbed her purse and walked toward the front door while stuffing her panties in her purse. She slipped out through the back slider. Marco followed in disgust.

His expression changed to a big smile as he looked poolside to see his best friend, Miles, sitting on a lounge chair, his fingers interlocked and resting on the top of his head.

'Nice place ya got here, Marco.'

'Thanks, brotha.' Marco reached in for a handshake. 'Got a great deal on it.'

'Yeah?'

'Remember that fucker I invested fifty grand with, only to lose most of it in the end?'

'Oh yeah, did he die?'

'This is his fuckin house, man!'

'No shit?'

'Yup, drowned right there in that pool. So when I heard, I ran right to his family. Gave them a long sob story. They felt so guilty they gave me the house for pennies.'

Miles laughed. 'You always were good at shit like that.'

'I think they wanted out so bad, they were happy to sell it to me, turnkey, furniture and all.'

Suddenly the bug zapper sounded with a loud "ZAP". Something rather large had hit the electrified wire. A frying noise followed for several seconds. Miles and Marco looked at each other and spoke simultaneously.

'Good one!'

'So, come on in, I'll show you around real quick, then let's go gamble.'

Marco wrinkled his nose.

A powerful odour had crept across the yard. It was as if someone had taken a week old steak from out of a garbage can, rotten and full of maggots, marinated it in cat urine, and just chucked it onto a grill.

'Damn can you smell that?'

'Yeah man, what is it?'

They looked around for the source but the only thing it could have been emanating from was the bug zapper. It was still crackling. Eventually Marco shrugged.

'Probably a dragon fly, there seems to be a lot of them here. Come on, I need a shower.'

An hour later both men sat in Marco's Corvette. Black, sleek, polished and cleaned with care. The car was Marco's baby and he treated it better than any other possession. Beer bottles in hand, they weaved in and out of traffic on "95" and slowed only when they hit the known "cop-hotspots". Marco slipped his Metallica CD into the stereo and both started singing wildly. When Marco finished his beer, the bottle went out the car at ninety miles an hour to either smash on the highway, or most likely, hit an unsuspecting car; Miles handed him another. 'Take this exit!' he shouted.

Marco knocked the Corvette down a gear and they were both forced back by the abrupt deceleration. The exit was clear and he sped up through the "stop", narrowly missing two cars. Miles looked back and laughed with delight as both cars swerved wildly and ran into each other. The sounds of metal on metal, horns blasting, and oscillating car alarms, were quickly left behind. Macro wasn't familiar with the road they were on, but he still drove it like he was on a Formula One race track. Ahead he saw a tractor-trailer slowing down for the closing gates of a railroad. Marco and Miles exchanged drunken looks and with a smirk, Marco pushed his Corvette hard and swerved to overtake the truck. A loud air-horn burst through the air, followed by the sound of a tractor-trailer desperately trying to stop. The gates were almost halfway closed and Marco focused on the gap.

He could make it.

Miles was screaming and punching the air. He followed the line of the railroad, to the bright light of a freight train moving at high speed towards them. It sounded its horn in unison with the tractor-trailer. Miles looked back to see the truck begin to jack-knife. All of a sudden this didn't seem like such a great idea. Worried, he looked at Marco, who paid him no attention.

The train sped toward them.

The trailer of the truck was now next to the cab, and coming up at them, fast.

Marco squinted and pushed harder on the accelerator.

The car hit the gate, ripping a wing mirror off; it flew in and smacked Miles in the head.

He ducked down dazed. A blinding pain behind his eyes.

Marco's heart raced and his vision slowly tunnelled

The train bore down on them, like a raging elephant.

Horns blared from all around and then there was an almighty crash, as truck and train met in a blazing inferno.

In that split second, time seemed to stop.

Miles was semiconscious, blood pouring from his left temple.

Marco, hands locked to the wheel, looked up and saw a tunnel of light....

The screen displays a classic 1960s horror typographic entitled:

"Revolting Tales: Episode Three"

A camera slowly pans towards an outside pool, leaves are blowing in the breeze. It's bright; we hear the sound of water movement, the camera moves up, and the view shifts to a panoramic of the pool. Sitting on an inflatable chair, a large man basks in the sun. Around the pool, insects of all descriptions fly in and.
One large insect hits the water.
It helplessly tries to escape.

The camera slowly zooms in as the large dragonfly fights to break the water's grasp...

Episode Three:

Dragonfly

'Come on, breathe....

   You can do it....

   Come on big fella, show me a sign....

   .....There ya go! Well hello. Welcome back, little buddy.'

Sal blew a tender breath toward his finger where a staunch dragonfly now perched. He was trying to help it dry off its wet little wings after it had nose-dived into his pool.

Sal looked with amazement, wonder, and a feeling of accomplishment, after rescuing the lifeless insect.

Sal had saved many dragonflies this summer and countless summers before.

He loved them dearly. He was intrigued by their physiology, their intense colour, their position at the top of their respective food chain. The speed they had and the ability to hover like a helicopter, how they ate thousands of pesky mosquitoes. He hated those fucking mosquitoes. They always bit him in places he could not reach.

Sal was a rather hefty man. A hairy man. A fat man...

This wasn't always the case, but after making millions in the hedge fund market, he retired early and enjoyed life to excess.

It was after his wife took him for a few million; he'd bought the place in Greenwich, Connecticut and secluded himself from everyone.

Sal didn't have any human contact, other than running into the maid now and then, and an occasional delivery boy from the local Peapod Supermarket.

He grew bitter over the entire world and at the age of 65, he was completely content living in his little bubble and saving dragonflies.

He watched as the little creature wiped its eyes and head off. Sal loved the beauty of its head, metallic looking - reflective. He could see the curvature of its iron looking mouth that came to a daggering point. He knew this was to bite and crush the heads off those menacing flies in mid-air, suck out there inner life force, and discard the rest of their bodies, simply by letting go of them. He often wished he could do that to the pesky people in his life.

He checked the time, another hour and his favourite television show would be on. Last week was amazing. It was like the end of the world or something. Man against beast. He couldn't quite remember the entire episode. To be honest, he couldn't remember if he'd had breakfast that morning. What he could recall was this. A group of soldiers, up a mountain somewhere in Colorado, but instead of desert there was water for miles. These soldiers were fighting hordes of animals. It was gruesome. Soldier trying to reload got impaled by charging elks, or ripped apart by groups of wolves. A guy, probably their leader, got his head swiped off by a bear. Hundreds of men were butchered and mutilated – and actually it was almost a metaphor for the nasty way he'd lived his life.

You see, Sal's life was opulent by even the richest of standards. His multi-million dollar bank accounts earned him more interest in a month, than the average person earned in ten years. To look at him now, you wouldn't even think he had been the most prestigious and respected man in financial institutions across the world. Respect and feared. He'd made most of his money ensuring that idiots with money to invest never made more of theirs. He conned, he cheated, he lied, and he never did enough to get caught. Investments were carefully managed, money hidden in offshore accounts, even his bitch of a wife, who managed to get her hands on a few million, had no idea just how rich he was. Her lawyer did. And because of his silence, he actually ended up with more than she did. That always made Sal laugh. Everyone had their price; everyone was corruptible.

Sal recalled the day he sat in front of the dumb fuck with five hundred thousand to invest. The most money he'd ever had in his life. Sal smiled, pushed him subtly towards the managed fund – his fund. Oh it was hidden, layered in fake company, after fake company. He had assured him that the risks were minimal, hell, he'd even been kind enough to point out the risks. And when the investment disappeared – as it was always going to do - and the offshore oil company collapsed, because it never really existed, Sal did his best to comfort the schmuck, using a stage-show of compassion that did very little to actually comfort him. Sal even considered giving him a cheque for fifty thousand dollars of his own money, because he actually felt sorry for him – of course he didn't – but he had thought about it. That counted, right?

He read unemotionally that the man had jumped from a thirty-floor high-rise, holding both his kids. Sal's only reaction was one of vindication.

He'd been absolutely right *not* to have wasted the fifty-thousand on him.

Sal had read many books on dragonflies and although he was far from a religious man, he often fantasized and hoped he would be reincarnated into one.

He walked through the pool toward the stairs while giving a helping blow onto his little buddy's wings to help them dry quicker. As he reached the pool steps, the dragonfly fluttered its wings and flew up off his finger.

Sal looked with wonderment as the dragon fly hovered directly in front of his eyes. Sal was confident they were having a symbiotic moment. The damn thing was thanking him. He was sure of it.

Sal reached for the pool stairs and the dragonfly slowly helicoptered away.

Sal was pleased with himself as he took one step up the ladder.

Without warning a strong burning pain started in his right arm and radiated up to his chest.

He clenched it and everything went black…

Darkness…

* * *

Sal had no perception of time.

When he finally awoke, it was with that feeling that he'd probably been asleep far too long.

Dazed and disorientated, he tried to regain focus, without much success. Eventually his brain was assaulted by an array of dazzling, intense colours. Blends of greens in a fusion of spectrum he could somehow see separated through octagonal shapes.

Hundreds of them.

He tried to blink but could not.

They were so brilliant but not painfully bright. It was quite "Peter Max".

He recalled the time he'd hallucinated with LSD, in the 60s, and how for six hours his entire surroundings were made up of brilliant colours.

He began to look from side to side, amazed at how the colours were changing from green, to brown.

He looked up to see intense vivid blue with plumes of bright fluffy white.

He tried to reposition himself, and when he did, he heard an intense fluttering noise. It startled him at first because it continued to happen every time he tried to move his arms.

It repeated several times until suddenly he felt his whole body move.

It felt amazing.

He decided to give his arms one good thrust and quickly discovered he was lifting completely off the ground. He kept the movement going and was amazed how effortless it was. As he ascended higher and, while looking down, he realized the brilliant green was in the shape of an oak leaf. He looked around to see the browns resembled tree bark.

Astonishment.

Excitement.

Elation.

He was overwhelmed by everything around him.

He now suddenly realised beyond all hope, his dream had came true.

Or maybe it was just a dream?

Maybe he was on the operating table or in a drug-induced coma. In any event, it didn't matter; it was fucking awesome.

He fluttered higher, forward, sideways, lower.

The colours were brilliant.

Jesus Christ, maybe there is life after death. Maybe I'm moving toward a brand new destiny?

Sal then fluttered right and found himself facing the most brilliant light he had ever seen.

Ultraviolet.

It was amazing.

He became obsessively drawn to it.

And so that's what he did.

It must be that spiritual light people always say they see after dying.

As he got closer he heard an intense humming.
That's not humming…
It sounds like fluttering!
It's got to be other dragonflies.
They're calling for me….I must go toward it.
…..It's so warm,
…So beautiful….
So…

* * *

… Miles and Marco looked at each other and spoke simultaneously. 'Good one!'

Library books of the dead...

Sandra maintained a respectable distance beside Lou, holding the latest volume of books in her arms. Lou's library was extensive, the expanse of which was immeasurable. Since the dawn of time, he'd kept meticulous records, and those who came into his realm were catalogued and filed. Each book told the life story of the newest occupant of Hell. The cover made from their own skin, the pages hand pressed and pulped from their sinew and bone, the writing within formed from their blood: they were now denizens of the underworld – the faceless and anonymous. It was their book, their life, and now it belonged to Lou for eternity.

He paused as he found the section he was looking for and he held out his hand. Sandra in turn passed him one, first checking the spine one last time, as if she might have made a mistake: Sandra never made mistakes. He took the book and pushed it into the waiting hole with care. As it slotted into its position, an eye opened on the spine. Its movement was rapid, it blinked many times, and again it rapidly moved around observing them both. As the two of them walked back in the direction they had come, eyes began to open along the spines of all the other books.

It was a ritual he enjoyed.

The very special occupants were hand-placed in the library by Lou himself.

It was an honour.

The screen displays a classic 1960s horror typographic entitled:

"Revolting Tales: Episode Four"

The screen focuses in on Billy Mason as he is shown into the office of a smart looking older man.
He gets up and shakes Billy's hand and they both sit.

The camera then zooms in to Billy...

Episode Four:

Escaping Matilda – (Part Two)

Doctor Natas Striker moved some papers on his tidy desk and, when satisfied, removed his glasses and smiled. Directly opposite him sat Billy.

'So how are you feeling?' He pulled a gold pen from his pinstriped suit and flipped over a notepad.

'Terrible.' Billy sighed into his hands.

'I see,' remarked Doctor Striker, 'but specifically,' he encouraged.

'Light headed, sick to my stomach. Scared to sleep, scared to close my eyes.' Billy rubbed his face.

Doctor Striker made brief notes. When Billy stopped, he paused.

'Anything else?'

Billy shrugged. 'Isn't that enough?'

'Well, not really. I mean it's a general list of symptoms, but I need you to be more specific, son. Let's try another tactic. Tell me about the dreams.'

Billy shuddered.

'But in detail, everything you remember, the imagery, the way they made you feel, the content. Play it back in your mind like a television show. If you feel uncomfortable put it on pause. Remember you're quite safe here.' He saw the fear in Billy's eyes and smiled a little. 'Don't forget, Billy, dreams are nothing more than series of images, ideas, emotions, and sensations, that occur involuntarily in the mind during certain stages of sleep, honestly, they can't hurt you.'

Billy didn't seem convinced, so he continued.

'Dreams are, in essence, individual mental activities, usually in the form of an imagined series of events. Dreams can and do reveal a lot about us, so by expressing them, I can assist you in understanding their meaning. You understand?'

'Yeah.'

'Good, so let's start with the first time you started having these dreams.'

'Dream,' Billy corrected.

'A reoccurring dream?' He made a note.

Billy thought hard a moment. 'Well, yes and no. I mean, the same things tend to happen, there's this girl, she's always there, but the setting is a little different each time. Usually I end up back in this old house.'

Doctor Striker nodded, but didn't look up.

'The first time I remember was about a week ago, not long after I had the accident.'

'When you broke your ankle?'

'Yes.'

'Let's stay with that for a moment. The dreams started occurring soon after that?'

Billy nodded.

'I see, and how exactly did you break it?'

Billy squirmed a little. Doctor Striker waited patiently for a response.

'Playing soccer,' he replied.

'Hmm,' Doctor Striker put down his pen, interlocked his fingers and leant on his elbows. 'This isn't going to work if you're not honest with me, Billy.'

'I don't know what you're talking about.'

Striker leant forward a little. He smiled knowingly. 'Listen, Billy, I've been doing this a long time, I know when someone isn't being entirely honest with me. That might have been the story you told your mom, and I understand why, but that's not what you need to tell me. So let's try again, shall we, how exactly *did* you break your ankle?'

'In a car.' The words blurted out quicker than he could stop them. 'Please don't tell Ma.'

Striker picked his pen back up and looked down. 'Everything said here is confidential, Billy.'

'Well, the truth is, friends from college had borrowed a car and –'

'By borrowed, I assume you mean stolen?'

'Yeah,' Billy had the good grace to lower his head a little.

'Carry on.'

'Well, we were drinking. Harry took us to this abandoned house on Banbury Lane and while we were there, we all took turns in driving. Everything was great, until Harry drove into a tree.'

'And that was when you broke your ankle?'

'Uhuh, we strapped it up and then I went to the clinic the next day, they called Ma, so I had to make up a story.'

'Understandable. What type of tree?'

'I'm sorry?'

'What type of tree did you drive into?'

'I don't know. It was big though. Old. Branches went right into the ground, kind'ov drooping down low.'

'A willow?'

'Maybe.'

Striker sat back into his chair. 'That's very interesting, Billy. Willows often have stoloniferous roots; the smallest part can grow deep into the ground. A willow of significant age can have tendrils deep into the earth.'

Billy wasn't sure where this was leading. He said nothing.

'So, you left the house after the incident, and then you started having these dreams?'

'The very next night.'

'That's not a coincidence, is it Billy?' Striker made another note.

'I guess not.'

'We're really getting somewhere.' He put down his pad, clicked his pen and placed it back into his pocket.

'You think the accident caused them?'

'I think you've been lying about a lot of things, it's just possible that your unconscious mind is rebelling.'

Billy thought hard.

'I feel better having told you,' he answered honestly.

'That's a good start.' He smiled and then asked, 'Tell me about the little girl.'

Billy felt a chill down his spine at the mention of her. The room seemed to darken. Billy felt an odd pressure against his throat, an irritation he tried to brush away. He coughed but the pressure continued. His eyes followed a fly and he swiped at it. Doctor Striker noted with some satisfaction that he'd discovered a catalyst. His satisfaction turned immediately to concern as he noticed Billy's ridged posture in the chair.

'Billy?'

Billy's eyes glazed over and he fought hard for breath. The pressure on his throat continued in earnest and he began to grab at himself in panic. He felt his eyes bulging, as if some unseen hand was choking the life from him. He felt the muscles around his throat tighten and the very same nebulous hands he'd experienced previously were again pawing at him. He could only watch in horror as his shirt pulled itself out of his jeans. His belt snapped open and pulled itself through the loops. He saw Doctor Striker leave his chair quite suddenly and back away from him, fear and uncertainty wreathing his face. His jeans were yanked down to his ankles. Striker pushed himself as far into the corner of the room as he could, his fear had consumed him. He was shouting something, but Billy couldn't hear. He felt something thrust into his mouth, a ball or something similar, he bit down on it as hard as he could. And he watched in muted silence as the belt slowly uncurled. It straightened out in mid-air and just as quickly, it cracked down across Billy's bare thighs. Tears fell from his eyes and his screams were muted by whatever was in his mouth. Striker jumped as the belt rained down on the boy. He was screaming now, but as blow after blow continued to fall, the skin on his legs torn to shreds, Billy was no longer conscious of him or what he might be shouting.

Billy fought for air as the images in the room turned soft – indistinct - their focus shifting constantly. He wasn't sure now if what he was seeing was real or imagined. The pain he suffered was beyond anything that he could ever remember feeling. And then it stopped. The belt fell to the ground. The room became silent, save for Billy's snivelling and Doctor Striker's whimpering.

They were both paralysed in fear.

Billy's vision blurred, invisible restraints forced his head upright. Again he felt rough hands fondling him, and he cried out against it. Suddenly, behind him, he heard a soft giggle. He managed to twist his head just far enough to see. In the corner of the room stood Matilda. In her left hand was a letter opener, the one Billy had spotted on Striker's desk. In a blur of movement she was at him, they were so close he could smell her breath upon him, putrid and rank. She twisted her head and turned her black eyes to the quivering man, who was crouched down low. And with the same movement she leapt at him, her hand still holding the letter opener, and before Doctor

Striker could defend himself against her, she tore open his throat and face, spraying his blood and tissue across the desk. Striker gurgled and screamed, desperately trying to fight her off. He couldn't release himself from her grip, and as she rained blow after blow, she penetrated his eye until his strength finally failed him, as he succumbed to her onslaught, he fell with a heavy thud onto the desk. The blood had spewed across the room and covered Billy. Striker twitched as the blunt blade penetrated his brain, and Matilda continued her frenzied stabbing long after he had died.

Billy whimpered as Matilda raised herself to her full three-feet and jumped down off the desk.

'Whoopsy.' She giggled, pressing the weapon into his shaking hand. She leaned into his face and licked his nose.

Billy was conscious of an odd reverberation coming from all around him. He could feel it more than hear it. Matilda jumped into his lap and snuggled up to his chest. The restraints that held him released his neck and he could finally look down. Matilda was sucking her thumb and rocking gently on his lap. Then she looked up at him and smiled. Her hands shot up and held his face to hers.

In grotesque mimicry of Doctor Striker, Matilda said, 'Don't forget, Billy, dreams are nothing more than series of images, ideas, emotions, and sensations, that occur involuntarily in the mind during certain stages of sleep, honestly, they can't hurt you.' She cackled then held his face tighter, forcing their heads to touch.

'Bring me more!' she screamed and then he was alone, able to move, he stood shakily, Doctor Striker's body lay at an obtuse angle, blood dripped everywhere. The reverberation he heard snapped sharply into focus as he looked towards the door to the consulting room. It burst open. Two police officers rushed in, their weapons drawn. They stopped dead at the sight before them. Billy tried to speak but the only thing that came out was a gurgled murmur. His jeans still around his ankles. His face and body covered in Doctor Striker's blood. His hands still holding the envelope opener. Blood slowly dripped from its blunt edge.

Both officers were stunned for a moment, but one, a sergeant, stepped forward cautiously. 'Drop the weapon, son.'

Billy looked down at his hand and let it open, allowing the blade to fall.

'It wasn't me,' he managed to say in a quiet whimper, but before he could utter another word, the officer was on him, dropping him face down, forcing his arms behind his back. He felt cold steel snap against his wrists and then he blacked out.

The screen displays a classic 1960s horror typographic entitled:

"Revolting Tales: Episode Five"

A camera pans along a grubby alleyway. It passes a dumpster and we hear the sounds of movement. There's a crackling-electric sound as the camera catches the bottom half of a flickering neon sign which reads "Caesar Palace". The camera steadily zooms into a group of cats feeding from a bowl outside grease stained doors that reads "Staff Only".

As the camera pans around them, they eat with gusto. The door slowly opens, revealing a pair of legs. A grubby linen bag drops down. A Pair of male hands grabs a cat in each and forces them into the bag.

Some cats scatter, some continue to eat.

There is a sound off screen, a cough, a wheeze. The bag is pulled up and the owner of the legs disappears back behind the door.

The camera slowly pans to a hunched form, holding a dark object. The camera zooms in to a black cat with glowing green eyes….

Episode Five:

#9 with Broccoli

'Here, kitty, kitty, kitty!'

Gladice believed she was the saviour of unwanted cats. Gladice was also a trailer park baby. No one had bothered to explain to her parents that Gladice was actually incorrectly spelt, neither knew how to read or write anyway, so what did it matter?

She put down a pale of water and then poured from a twenty-five pound bag of this week's special at the local Uno-Dos-Quattro Mart "Yer Kitties choice" dry cat food. The food hit the linoleum kitchen floor, bouncing and rolling in several directions. Cats of all shapes, sizes, colours, and ages came running from every corner of the home.

The air filled with meows, whining, purrs, and hisses, as each ran on top of the mounding pile of cat food. They gorged all they could, only to stop momentarily to hiss and remind others of their claimed territory. The air was filled with an over powering odour of cat urine, cat faeces, rotting garbage, and decaying animal flesh.

The bag emptied, Gladice began to shuffle her way through the cat covered kitchen floor.

She spoke. 'Enjoy it my little sweets, it may be the last for a while. Kitty, kitty, kitty.'

She puckered her lips and made several kissing sounds.

Gladice headed for the door she always came and left from. Her breathing was raspy as was her voice. She believed it was caused by the years of smoking Raleigh 100 cigarettes. She refused to believe it was caused by the years of over powering ammonia from her little sweet excrements.

Her pendulum breasts swung freely from under the multi-coloured oversized T-shirt, which was once white. She wiped her nose with her wrist and followed up by itching at the clump of facial hair just below her left jaw. Her long scraggy un-brushed obtusely died burnt-orange hair resembled an old 1970s shag rug. Her brown stretch pants sported a huge *gunt*, which was shadowed only by a very pronounced camel-toe.

She never once looked at any of the sixty-six felines she housed in her home. If she did, she would clearly see most were emaciated, losing hair and had open and infected wounds from fighting each other. Some were limping, others fur-caked and clumped with dry faeces.

Gladice believed she was a rescuer of unwanted cats, but by the build-up of written warnings posted all over her property, along with posted health advisories that papered the front door, it was apparent to everyone but her, she was an animal hoarder.

Gladice was well aware Connecticut had a state statute for animal hoarding. She was aware the town health department was trying to get her evicted from her home, for numerous health violations: for the lack of wholesome air, build-up of cat excretion, urine over flow, open bags containing hundreds of empty cat food cans and a rotting assortment of God knows what else, along with mounds upon mounds of stacked up garbage.....oh, and no running water. She thought about the legal term they used and said under her breath, 'Inhabitable conditions? Ridiculous!'

None of that concerned her at this moment because "they" were all crazy. She loved her cats. She rescued them. She saved them. They were her little sweets.

She reached for the door while kicking the wall trim with the tips of her slippers in order to remove the caked on dried cat excrement that had quickly built up on them. She swiftly opened the door and began to lightly kick away several of her sweets in order to keep them from following. When she was confident none of them would get caught in the door, she slammed it shut - hard.

The quick sharp sound of a bolt being slid in place followed.

Gladice needed an extra latch because the door would not stay closed on its own.

Caesar was a large black male tomcat. His hair was shiny and well kept.

Out of all the cats in the home, he was the largest and healthiest. This was because he was in charge. Caesar, with his penetrating green eyes, was the alpha-male. He ate first, drank first, slept where he wanted, and fucked who he pleased.

Caesar stared at the door Gladice had just closed. He looked with curiosity and contemplation from his King's lair located on the back of a large lime green coloured recliner. It was strategically located in the adjoining room. There were three rooms in total.

The kitchen was very small and had limited counter space. That was because every inch of it was covered with piles of empty cat food cans, newspapers, mounds of mail, empty soda cans and coffee cups. There were countless piles of garbage bags filled with used kitty litter. A refrigerator stood in the corner, never to be open again, since the power went out months ago. Its purpose now was simply a makeshift mortuary; a place for Gladice to put her poor deceased sweets in when they passed away.

The living room, Caesar's realm was cleaner because he demanded it.

Lastly there was a small bathroom. The toilet was empty; the cats had drunk it dry months ago. The tub had been used as a litter box but now was simply too full to use. There were several cat carcasses mixed in. Their deathbed caused by many different afflictions, but mostly because they had eaten the excrement from the tub.

Caesar heard the sliding bolt. He wasn't quite sure what it was, but he knew it happened every time she came in, and when she left. He also realised that Gladice had not been coming there as often as she used to and the food and water wasn't as plentiful as weeks past.

He received reports from his lieutenants - four in all- grey males, domestic short hairs, sitting in unison, two on each arm rest- just below their King. They had reported many of his flock were ill and starving. He knew if Gladice cut rations any further, he would lose more and he didn't want that to happen.

He reflected back to when he was on the outside, living high on the hog while growing up near a dumpster. Food was plentiful at "Caesar's Palace". The Chinese owners used to leave the dumpster open and load it with all sorts of tasty food. They would even leave it on plates for them, but that food was always left for the elder cats. Caesar puzzled over why all the elders who moved up to the plate dinner service always disappeared a day or two later.

He recalled how quickly things changed when the Chinese restaurant had closed down and the dumpster went empty. Caesar narrowly escaped the cannibal games the elders had to establish in order to save the feral cat colony from starvation. It was usually the elders or the very young who lost but he recalled when he was picked to compete to the death, paired up with another tom his age but much larger, being on his back and not able to break free from a dying throat hold. He thought he was about to become dinner when his opponent broke the hold and suddenly scattered with all the other colony members.

It was then that he heard her for the very first time

'Oh! Don't worry, honey; I got you now, my poor sweets.'

He appreciated the save, but after years living in this three room dungeon, he would take freedom and the possibility of being eaten over this incarceration any day.

Caesar wanted out and he would do anything to make that happen.

Anything…

Gladice did not return for some time.

A lot can happen in three weeks.

His heartbeat stopped. The young Persian lay dead.

The old grey tom let go of his throat hold. There was a moment of silence as he looked up at his king. All spectators' eyes followed.

Caesar gracefully jumped from his throne to the floor, landing on all fours. He stood tall and scanned the entire room, then walked to the winner. He stood inches from him and glared into his eyes. A brief contest of wills ended with old grey submitting, lowering his head to a bow.

Caesar turned and with a tiger's roar reached down and tore a leg off the Persian. As he walked away, old grey tore off the other.

Frenzy followed. The room filled with deadening growls, hisses, and whines.

Within seconds there was nothing left but clumps of fur, and spatters of blood, being licked up by two emaciated kittens.

Two days later the sun began to peek through a crack in the permanently closed curtains. Caesar awoke to a familiar sound. The door opened and in shuffled Gladice.

'Mommy's here my little sweets.'

Caesar's hopes for quality food were quickly diminished, when he saw her carrying a small ten-pound bag of dried cat food. He was angry. Angry at the constantly dwindling food. That his flock were looking to him to fix it. Angry that he had to continually eat rotten cat flesh to stay alive.

This was it.

He'd had enough.

It was time for battle.

Caesar motioned to his lieutenants. They moved in unison without hesitation, breaking off in different directions; each gathered members of their squad as they moved to their assigned battle positions.

Caesar jumped from his throne and landed in battle stance.

His target was clearly in sight. Vivid green eyes stared with murderous intentions.

Unsuspecting, Gladice ripped open the bag and began to pour.

'Oh, you must be starving, my poor little sweets. Mommy's here, here, here, kitty, kitties.'

Instinct and the hairs standing erect on her arms told her something was wrong. Abruptly she stopped pouring and looked up and around.

None of the cats were coming like they always did, time and time again.

She was puzzled.

'Kitty, kitty?'

She cradled the bag of food in her left arm and started to walk toward the living room, when in an instant, Caesar jumped onto the corner of the counter knocking several cans from it. He was inches from her.

It startled her.

She froze.

'Caesar!'

He began to growl, a guttural sound that started in his tail and built momentum, until his entire body shook. With a loud hiss, he leapt at her, impaling claws from all four paws deeply into her sagging breasts. He took most of her lower lip into his mouth and bit down deeply. Her high raspy scream mimicked his angry whine.

The attack knocked Gladice off balance. She stumbled and tripped over several bags of garbage, falling back and hitting her head on the handle of the refrigerator. She fell like a two-hundred pound sack of cat food and the fridge door opened.

Gladice briefly wrestled with the rotting maggot ridden cat carcasses that poured out from the refrigerator. The older dried carcasses bounced as they fell, but the latter ones, at the point of expanding gaseousness and internal liquefaction – their little arms and legs poking outward, bloated like balloons - burst on impact, releasing putrid, rancid thickly viscous liquid all over her face. This allowed hundreds of fresh maggots and casters to slip easily down her throat and up her nose. The smell and shock caused her to vomit uncontrollably just before passing out.

Gladice awoke from pain.

Her first conscious thought was the overpowering odour of the decomposing cats. She coughed and spluttered, reaching up to wipe the rancid fluid from her face and eyes. A horrific pain quickly masked the taste of putrefied cat internal organs. Her eyes were stinging. Things were blurry as she lifted her head to see. Pain gave way to horror as she saw the murderous swarm approaching her. Her sweets were out for blood. They covered her entire body. She was amazed how quiet they were. She realised then with dread, she'd only ever witnessed it when they were all eating. A stabbing pain in her abdomen caused her to scream. She looked down to find her sweets had torn open her stomach cavity, and were pulling out her intestines.

She feverishly tried to push them away and saw that three of her finger from one hand and a thumb from the other had already been chewed off.

Terror, panic, and screams prompted enough adrenaline for her to spin her body around. She lifted to her hands and knees and began to crawl for the door; feverishly pushing, grabbing, punching, kicking, biting, and throwing cats aside.

Caesar was back on the corner of the kitchen counter, strategically assessing the battle. He looked to the reserve units standing in formation waiting for the order to attack.

He gave a lion's roar and two formations moved forward and charged her.

She was a tough old bird.

He didn't think she would have survived the fall. But she had managed to get to the door and reach up and grabbed the handle. As she began to stand, the door opened. Caesar realised it was all or nothing. He turned to the last reserve units and ordered them all to attack.

Caesar turned back to the battle and hissed with displeasure.

Gladice was now standing on the other side of the door, one hand holding in her intestines, the other throwing an emaciated cat against the wall. She kicked the last of his warriors back in the room.

She looked directly at him.

He looked back at her.

She knew…

The door slammed shut.

Caesar howled. *No, No NO! How can this be! This can't be happening… I've been defeated…It's over.* He bowed his head. Not knowing what to do next, his mind went blank. Seconds passed, and then he heard a familiar noise.

It was a creaking door.

He looked up quickly, to see the door opening slightly.

A burst of excitement as his first thought came to him.

He hadn't heard the sliding bolt sound.

She forgot….or didn't have the strength to lock the door….this is it!

With a roar that said: *Follow me!* Caesar charged for the door with his entire army behind him. He was going to finish this once and for all.

As he reached the door, his minions waited. He put a paw through the gap and pried the door open enough for them all to escape. It was dark beyond. He cautiously stopped at the threshold. He smiled to himself. His ability to see in the dark was his power. He charged into the darkness, his flock followed.

Clap, clap!

The lights came on in the room.

It briefly blinded him.

In the middle of the room Gladice was lying on her side, propped up on one elbow.

She clapped again, and several guillotine doors located in sequence on each adjacent wall opened in unison.

Caesar and his army slowed to an abrupt stop. There was silence.

The two of them, Gladice and Caesar, eye to eye; but instead of seeing defeat in her eyes, he saw confidence. She smiled a wicked evil smile.

For the first time since he'd started the assault, King Caesar was unsure.

Gladice had a twinkle in her eyes that frightened him.

What was it she knew?

A soft growl, followed by another, made Caesar back up.

His flock backed with him.

Bright eyes appeared from inside the guillotine cages.

Many pairs of eyes.

Slowly moving closer.

Closer…

Until thirty pit bulls of all shapes and sizes rushed through the guillotine doors.

Their panting jaws dripping with saliva and anticipation.

'Dinner time, my little muffins!'

Gladice believed she was also the saviour of unwanted pit bulls….

Wastepaper Basket

Sandra was just putting the final penmanship on the latest volume of books for Lou to file, when the door to her office opened quietly. Unaware, she smiled as she gauged the quality of her work. The cover looked amazing, a top-notch job. The skin had bonded particularly well to the bone underlay. She ran a finger around its edge. It was perfectly razor-sharp. She really was good at her job.

A soft purr distracted her and she looked up in irritation straight into the eyes - or eye - of a black cat - one was bright-red, the other missing. For the longest time they stared at each other. Eventually the cat said: 'Sandra, could you please cancel my three o'clock.'

Lou.

She rolled her eyes and nodded. 'Of course.'

The cat showed yellowish fangs – its approximation of a smile.

'Don't you want to know what I'm doing instead?'

'No.' She looked down at the book she was working on, ignoring his attempts to engage her. A black paw playfully tapped at her pen. Without pause, she grabbed him by the scruff of his neck and unceremoniously dropped him; he landed on all fours and instantly sprang back up and knocked paperclips and other stationery across the otherwise tidy desk.

Sandra lifted both hands in irritation. 'Busy, Lou!'

He grabbed a paperclip and flicked it into the air and rolled onto his back. Sandra sighed, picked up the meat clever that just happened to be beside her chair, and without pause, brought it down hard. The cat's head flew into the air, and landed perfectly into the wastepaper basket. The body flipped and bucked, spraying blood everywhere. Sandra picked it up by the tail and dropped it too, into the basket. The head looked up at her. Laughing, he said, 'Oh that was fucking great! You really know how to please me, Sandra. I love you.'

With a smirk, she simply closed the lid.

The screen displays a classic 1960s horror typographic entitled:

"Revolting Tales: Episode Six"

The camera pans slowly around a full bar and comes to a stop. Groups of girls, scantily clad, are dancing to a country band playing off in one corner. We hear bouts of laughter and the camera pans toward the bar and then slowly zoomed in to a lone man sitting at one end, leaning into his drink. The seat next to him is empty. As the back of the man slowly fills the screen, a woman slips in beside him, whispers something into his ear.

He looks at her startled, and then quickly downs his beer, drops some cash on the bar, and they leave...

Episode Six:

It's a Girl!

The pain could be compared to? Well... Nothing.

His stomach felt like someone had hold, and was spinning it, the same way you close a garbage bag before securing it with a twist tie.

Smitty's backside was sore from sitting on the toilet for the last several hours. It burned - stung. He grumbled to himself... trying not to think about it. Should he just not bother wiping? Even wiping it with the softest most luxurious toilet paper ever known to man, the kind the Queen of England probably used, was still like wiping with course sandpaper, enriched with poison oak.

He started to wipe.

... like fibreglass!

... rusty box-cutter blades!

... no, needles!

... live pissed-off hornets, earwigs, and wasps!

... molten fucking lava!

... *FUCK!*

He feared trying to leave the bathroom because of the last incident away from it.

He hoped someone would come soon and didn't care about the projectile vomit and shit they would see all over the house and on everything. Furniture, walls, floors....his fish tank.

At least the sink was close enough to the toilet he could keep himself hydrated.

'Amazing,' he said out loud.

He could not believe one person could vomit and shit so much.

Another volley of stomach pain made him buckle over and scream.

Scream – like a proper scream. Not a clutch yourself and curse, or a low groan.

No a scream. Like that Nazi guy at the end of "Raiders of the Lost Ark" when the ghost came out of the box; that scream... One of anguish, pain, and terror! He was clueless as to what was causing it.

He began reflecting back through the past twenty-four hours.

He thought about breakfast but quickly stopped as he began feeling nauseated at the thought of food.

He smiled for a moment.

He thought of Jenn….

Yeah baby…. The hot chick that "picked him up" at the local bar. Never had a girl whisper a pick up line like that before. In fact, he'd never had a girl pick him up before.

His pleasurable memory of great stranger sex dissipated to the immediate reality he was going to vomit and shit simultaneously once again.

And he did.

It spewed from his mouth so forcefully it reached the adjoining shower stall, spattering back and hitting everything around him, to include his feet.

The sight and feel of his warm vomit made him vomit again. The smell was so overpowering it watered his eyes. The colours, like the pain, were like no other. The lighter colour looked like abscessed puss, the reds were more of a purple tint. The brown was identical to his shit.

It was horrifying.

The volume of vomit and shit coming out of him had not dissipated in the least.

He couldn't for the life of him figure it out, but knew it was not good. He also knew that at some point it had to end, just because there couldn't be anything left inside to come out. He thought about getting the phone. Thought about calling a doctor, an ambulance, a fucking priest!

The taste in his mouth was so bitter and foul, he desperately tried keeping it closed after each upchucks so he wouldn't have to smell it. He then realized he had a pack of mints in his short pants pocket. He reached down into his right pocket and was quickly relieved they were still there.

Smitty quickly tore open the pack and grabbed two mints and put them together. They were now two mints….two mints in one.

He popped them feverishly into his mouth and began chewing them.

It was a refreshing sweet treat he thought as he swallowed.

Before they could get past the oesophagus, Smitty's stomach twisted.

He screamed painfully and this time began to uncontrollably cry.

The toilet water slashed up and coated his balls and ass cheeks with liquid shit. It continued to pour out of his ass like a kinked garden hose that had suddenly became unkinked.

He could only sit there and let it drip from him.

The toilet paper was long gone, which was a blessing as it felt like his sphincter was now the size of a female baboon's ass in heat.

Too weak now to do anything but drool and dribble from all orifices, he continued to hope someone would come…anyone…even a Jehovah's Witness would be welcome at this point.

He thought it was getting close to mail delivery.

Smitty figured since he always heard the squeaking storm door open and slam shut everyday due to the mail man placing the mail between doors - he could yell out for help and hopefully be saved from this shit kicking, vomit volley nightmare.

Without any warning he felt another volley of vomit coming. But it was different this time. His stomach felt full.

How could that be! There can't be anything else left.

He took a deep breath and prepared for it.

But something new happened.

He couldn't breathe.

He felt movement in his chest, in his throat.

The pain was unbearable.

He grabbed at his neck and began to thrash wildly with his legs.

The muscles of his neck pulsed at odd intervals.

Rhythmic intervals.

Wide eyed he had an odd compunction to gag and push. Red faced and without any real understanding why, he followed that compunction to push with all his might - and screamed as a mass of blood and intestines burst through his sphincter landing in the toilet bowl.

A short gag reflex began again and this time, Smitty passed out.

He was sitting slumped over. His jaw rested on his chest.

His neck began to swell, veins became pronounced, his neck muscles moved arithmetically like a snake's body.

His mouth slowly opened wide….then even wider. His jaw dislocated and his mouth opened to disfigurement. It remained open for several seconds spewing a milky white thick liquid that slowly oozed from one corner of his mouth.

Four tiny fingers reached out from within and gripped his upper lip.

Another four tiny fingers reached out and grabbed his lower lip.

Smitty's mouth widened a bit more. Bones and cartilage snapped and popped.

A head slowly appeared pushing its way through the tiny hole, which was rapidly becoming much larger.

Blood sprayed and the lower jaw finally gave way, snapping, hanging obtusely. An infant slipped out and landed in Smitty's lap. Still attached to the umbilical cord. Smitty involuntarily choked as the placenta lodged in his throat.

Eventually it too fell with a wet-thump.

It was a normal, healthy baby girl.

Seven pounds, three ounces.

She lay in the warmth of his lap, covered in thick black goo of blood and shit. Eventually, when she had the strength to move she flopped herself onto the floor. Shakily she stood, her tiny back arched. Bone burst through her shoulders and tiny wings unfolded themselves. Her screams were gurgled and she writhed in pain as the skin split. Eventually they unfurled and she extended them. She licked herself clean and then rested for a moment, gathering the strength she needed. Tiny hands pulled her up to his lap again, and black feathered soaked wings flicked slime across the room. The infant reached up and pulled lumps of flesh from the gaping hole she'd emerged from. And tiny teeth ripped small pieces off and with gusto she fed until there was nothing recognisably left of Smitty.

She slept for a while after feeding, and when she awoke, her wings dry and able to lift her, she dove into the toilet as it flushed.

* * *

Joe Cocker's "Feelin' alright" played loudly from the jukebox as she walked through the bar-door.

A dapper young asshole stood leaning against the pool table drinking a Singapore Sling. He quickly moved toward her.

'Hey baby, what's your sign?' he slurred. Doing his best to stand on one spot, but the world kept him moving.

'Excuse me?' she replied with a frown.

'Ya know, your astrological sign…. I'm faeces.' He laughed drunkenly at his own joke.

She pushed him away. 'Get away, creep.'

She was not interested.

The bartender caught her eye and he waved at her. 'The usual, Jennifer?'

She nodded at him.

He shot out an arm. 'He's right over there.'

'Thanks, Lou.' And she moved with purpose to the guy sitting alone at the end of the bar.

She adjusted herself and took the stool next to him.

He turned.

Their eyes met.

He was pleased and showed that pleasure with his best sexy "let's fuck" smile.

She returned the look and reached over and whispered in his ear. 'I'm going to fuck you so hard you'll feel like I knocked you up.'

He laughed.

He'd never heard that one before….

The screen displays a classic 1960s horror typographic entitled:

"Revolting Tales: Episode Seven"

The picture fades into a view of a shop front. The name:
"Lou's Bait & Tackle, Groceries, Toy Store & Computer Repair"

The door opens and we hear a bell. The camera follows a man and a boy as then enter, inside we see various people browsing. The man walks up to the counter and smiles as the owner looks up.

'Hey, Lou.'

The boy walks over to a selection of soft toys, as the man and the owner talk, and the camera follows him. He looks up at the chiming of the doorbell, and as the camera follows his gaze, a young girl walks in. She smiles at him as she walks past...

Episode Seven:

Jerky

'Go ahead, stick it in….'

'Not too deep though…. you don't want to make her piss, now do ya?'

'That's it, now reach in with your forefinger and keep it just above the tip.'

'Jesus Christ! Slow down and stop shaking so much, you don't want to ruin her meat.'

'Now go right up the middle with it and try to get it up to her throat.'

'There ya go, good job, son.'

Jimmy Pirocchi looked down at his son with admiration and congratulated him on his first deer kill and field dressing of a young doe…..a deer….a female deer.

He reached over and shook the top of his head knocking his hat off.

'You're a man now, son.'

Lorrenzo didn't appear to be as happy as his dad thought he would be.

A shy 14-year old loner, who had been having some social issues in school, not quite fitting in, and not wanting to make friends - he often appeared timid and distant.

His father refused to accept the fact his kid had "issues" and believed that hunting would bring "the man out in him."

'Do you think she suffered, Dad?' Lorrenzo asked with a slightly saddened tone.

Jimmy quickly stood erect.

'Son, these are stupid animals. They're not people, their brains are not like ours. They simply eat, shit and fuck.'

Jesus fucking Christ, boy, it's food! It's survival of the fittest!

His increased angry tone quickly decreased to a monotone composure.

'We are the predators here, son.' He pointed at the doe, 'and that is our prey.'

Lorrenzo looked up at his dad and put on the best smile he could, then shook the top of his head in acknowledgement. He knew, as much as he did not like hunting, his dad did, and if this pleased him then by all means, he was going to do it to the best of his ability.

'I guess we need to work on your bow skills though, huh, kiddo?' They both chuckled.

'Yeah, Dad. I guess we do.' Another simultaneously chuckle.

As they dragged the small doe down the trail together the conversation continued but faded with distance.

'Three arrows is way too many, you need to get it down to a single shot.'

A small young spotted button buck stood off in the distance looking at the two hunters as they walked away.

He wasn't frightened. He didn't weep and he certainly wasn't mourning the loss of his mother.

No sir, he was just downright pissed off!

As he stood there expressionless, his eyes slowly narrowed and the expression morphed to a look of dire revenge. His black eyes darkened and went wide. His upper lip lifted slightly, as he sniffed the air for the two human's scent.

He appeared to want to remember it....

The pan sizzled when the butter hit the hot frying pan.

'Almost ready, son.'

Jimmy bent over to sniff a large piece of venison steak from his son's first doe kill. It would taste all the sweeter because of the fact Lorrenzo had killed it, and Jimmy had instructed him – and instructed him well. He was quite proud of himself, feeling a sense of accomplishment at breaking the kid out of his shell. There was nothing wrong with Lorrenzo that a father couldn't fix with some life skills; and what better skills to learn than hunting?

The pan continued to sizzle and the delightful smell drifted upwards, overwhelming Jimmy's sense, causing him to salivate. He swallowed and as he lifted his head, he became aware of movement that caught his attention. Outside the kitchen window he observed a small button buck standing at the edge of his property. It appeared to be staring right at him.

Jimmy smiled and thought, *There's one for the dinner table in a couple years.*

His attention turned to the television.

He half listened to the news broadcaster as he continued to cook supper.

...and coming up today in Oakland, a sad Christmas for one small child whose father dies in a bizarre electrocution accident by falling from his high rise apartment onto telephone wires, ten floors below. Witnesses say he was impaled on a telephone post in a crucifixion pose. Witnesses believe it was a sign from God.

Police still have no leads over the horrific, violent deaths of a young boy and two paramedics who were found locked in a storage room in Dewburry Elementary. Unconfirmed sources, close to the investigation, say that a Bobble-head Jesus was reportedly found clutched in one of the paramedic's hands. They are appealing for witnesses. You can contact Dewburry Investigators on the number at the bottom of your screen.

We talk with local residents in Bridgeport, Connecticut about the lack of movement in the eviction case of local hoarder Gladice Mcginty, despite several successful legal battles and various animal control orders.

Police are also appealing for witnesses to a shocking train derailment where a truck...

Jimmy turned his attention back to the venison and again bent over to give the meat a sniff.

That was when he felt an odd tingling sensation in his extremities.

Suddenly, his body went completely numb.

His eyesight went black.

All sounds disappeared.

...silence.

What seemed like only a moment in time Jimmy's hearing and eyesight slowly returned. Something however was wrong.

Very wrong.

All surrounding sounds had change. The sound of the sizzling pan was now juxtaposed with that of a babbling brook. The television broadcaster's voice was replaced with the resonance of fall wind, rustling leaves, and crows squawking as they flew overhead.

His sight blurrily came back into focus, but oddly only in black and white. He looked around and realised he was now in the woods. Dazed and confused he turned his head in the hope he would see familiar surroundings, but the lack of colours and clarity and the disorientation confused him. Conversely, he was amazed by how sharply his hearing and sense of smell increased. He could hear leaves crackle in the distance. He focused on a squirrel high up in an oak tree a hundred yards away. He watched while it scurried up the tree branch. Jimmy was even more amazed he could smell it.

It was definitely squirrel scent. He had killed and eaten many.

Jimmy also felt physically different. He was slightly uncomfortable with his stance. It was different and he was perplexed about it. He looked down, focusing on his feet.

….but they were no longer feet.

….they were hoofs.

His sight widened to see his whole body was covered in hair….deer hair.

Jesus Christ, I must be fucking dreaming. Yeah, I must have dozed off after dinner.

Confident it was all a dream, he relaxed a bit and decided to take it all in. His initial fear now simply turned to intrigue. He appreciated how alert and aware his senses were to his surroundings and he glanced down to the babbling stream in front of him.

He took in his reflection and chuckled to himself.

I'm a female deer... A fuckin doe!

He…

She stood there taking in nature's offers.

The intensity of bird songs.

The smell of acorns and field corn.

Sweet, succulent, ripe apples.

She slowly inhaled, allowing these new sensations to wash over her.

Suddenly her olfactory lobes were hit by an overpowering odour. Although she had never smelt anything like it before, it was oddly pleasing. She lifted her head and glanced around trying to pinpoint its location. Within seconds, she located its origin.

Thirty yards away stood a very large buck. It stood high and proud. His antlers were high and spread. She had never seen such a large deer.

Jimmy counted his antlers.
It was a hunter's trait.
A seven by seven. Christ, a fourteen pointer, if only I was him *in this dream.*

She glimpsed at his mouth to see his upper lip lift. Her admiration quickly turned to panic, because inside her, Jimmy knew that was a trait for rut....breeding season!

And it was breeding season; he was ready and coming right for her.

She tried to turn and run but as often in dreams she could not move her feet, hoofs, fast enough. Horrified at the thought of being mounted, she could only watch in terror at his approach.

And when he got close enough, he circled slowly around her.

Paralyzed in fear with Jimmy inside her screaming and cursing for her to move, she watched him circle.

She could only turn her head and watch as the buck approached.

In her mind, Jimmy thought, *Maybe if I say something, it will automatically turn to deer talk or some shit like that.*

'Hey, hey, hey, man! I'm a guy, don't do this!'

She was surprised to hear her voice was still, well, Jimmy's voice.

She looked at the buck for a response, but there was none.

The buck became ready.
His intention was clear...
...visibly.
'No! Please, oh Jesus, no!'

There was nothing more that could be said or done. She turned away, closed her eyes, and prepared for his inevitable mount. As she tightened with the anticipation of ripping pain, she heard a deep guttural voice.

'Do you remember me?'

She looked back at the buck. His lips moved as he repeated in a louder and angry voice, 'Do you remember me?''

Jimmy looked into his black eyes and had a flashback to the young button buck, standing in his yard.

Jimmy gasped.

Wake up, wake up, fucking wake up.

Jimmy repeated it over and over as hopelessly she watched him rear up and mount her.

She did not wake.

The pain was excruciating.

She thought she would pass out but she didn't.

With each thrust the intolerable pounding grew worse and then instantly, he was gone.

She opened her eyes hoping beyond all hope it was over, with a tremble she realised she was alone. The agony from her behind was excruciating but that became an instant memory, lost to another deeper and far more hideous pain. Inside her, Jimmy howled. It ripped through her with an intensity she (and he) had ever experienced before.

An agonisingly sharp, throbbing pain.

A far more unparalleled sensation.

She turned back and saw the horrific reality.

An arrow was imbedded deep into her left hip.

Jesus Christ, what the hell is happening here.

The pain numbed her hip. She tried to move but still could not.

Thinking she could maybe reach around and pull it out, Jimmy remembered how impossible that would be.

Her thoughts changed from remedy to overwhelming excruciating agony. Something just struck her right side and clearly penetrated her stomach. She looked to see another arrow protruding from her. She could see the fletching and about three inches of the shaft. She could feel the explosive bleeding filling her stomach cavity walls. She winced and turned her head away. Her eyes closed.

Sharp sudden pulsating agony forced her eyes open, and she turned to see the other side of her body, the second arrowhead stuck out about six inches. It was dripping with bright red blood that spurted from the exit hole with each pump of her heart. There were fragments of digested grass, leaves and bark hanging from the three razors sharp expandable prongs. A four inch long piece of intestine also protruded from the exit wound. It was torn open and dripping excretion.

She...

...could not move.

…could not pass out.

…could not block the excruciating pain that radiated throughout her body.

…needed to know where the arrows were coming from.

…looked around feverishly trying to pinpoint the shooter, but the hunter inside him knew how impossible that would be. She didn't understand, but Jimmy did. Every hunter's safety course taught, deer do not see in three dimensions, so their eyesight is extremely poor.

As she scanned the area a third arrow struck her shoulder, followed by another seconds later.

That arrow penetrated deep into her chest cavity.

Oh the horror.

She fell to the ground.

Hitting the ground with such force sent all the arrows deeper, tearing through all her inner organs.

She felt them slice open and tear, and burst, and bleed. All four were now exposed from the exit wounds and all had pieces of organs hanging from them.

Still paralyzed her breathing weakened.

They cried out in pain.

Jimmy thought of his son, wondering if he would turn out okay. To be the man Jimmy hoped he would become.

It was difficult to breathe now. He felt his lungs filling with blood, which spurted from his mouth with every exhale.

His sight was fading.

He knew this was it.

Hoping to wake up he again tried repeating:

Wake up now, you have to wake up now!

He heard leaves crackle. It was rhythmic. He knew it was something or someone walking toward him. However, he was lying on his side and did not have the strength to lift his head. What he could see was the beautiful fall summer sky. He felt the warm Indian summer breeze, the endless coloured leaves, all swaying in unison.

A figure came into sight but he was having difficulty making it out. He knew it had the shape of a person but the majority of the figure seemed transparent. He again realized it was due to the deer's two dimensional eye sight and subsequently recognised the figure was completely clothed in camouflage.

The figure was close. Standing directly over Jimmy's deer body.

Jimmy continued to focus his sight on the figure when he felt pressure on his head followed by the flash of unbearable pain. The figure was ripping the arrows out.

Jimmy felt his guts rip along with them.

Oh the horror!

Jimmy felt his body roll. He was now on his back. He saw the figure drop down to his knees and pull something from its body. He could not clearly make out what it was until he heard the ever so familiar "click". It was the sound of a locking field dressing knife blade.

Jimmy screamed.

He heard it loud and clear, as it reverberated throughout the forest.

He felt the knife penetrate his rectum. His screams continued now from the insufferable electrifying pain of the blade moving up through his groin, then his intestines, stomach and up to his throat. He just wanted to die. He begged Christ to let him die.

He looked up at the figure who reached up and pulled off his camo mask.

Jimmy focused on the face. He was begging him to stop.

And if his fear could not get any worse, the figure's face came into focus.

.....it was Lorrenzo.

Everything went black and silent.

Fade to Lorrenzo, dragging the doe down the path to his house.
Fade to the kitchen, as butter hits the frying pan.

Lorrenzo, several years older, looked down at the venison of the young doe his daughter Labella, just killed.

Labella flicked through the channels on the television in the adjoining room. She stopped out of boredom. There was nothing really worth watching anyway. A commercial was half through.

Labella turned off the television, but it stayed on. A man on the screen was waving frantically, pointing at her. She pointed to herself with a look of disbelief and he gave her the thumbs up. She giggled as he did a little Irish-jig, and as the advertising voice, loud and melodic continued his pitch, the odd looking man danced and danced and danced....

...but wait! If you act now, in addition to your new Gideon's Bible, we'll send you this Bobble-head Jesus. It goes anywhere you do....stick it in your car, let the kids take it to school, bring it on vacation, or have it with you as you're lounging by the pool....get one "Free" but only if you call in the next ten minutes. Pick up the phone and dial... 860-666-GABE

Lorrenzo looked back at the piece of tenderloin and gave it a sniff...

...and then something caught his eye, just outside the kitchen window.

The screen displays a classic 1960s horror typographic entitled:

"Revolting Tales: Episode Eight"

The camera's view is through CCTV of a teenage boy being interviewed in a room with a police officer. The angle is high and the police officer is seen walking around, gesticulating. He is shouting, but we don't hear what he is saying. The view shifts to a small television showing the same scene and zooms out until it passes through two people watching.

Their backs toward us .The camera pans around and we see a side profile of them both. A man and a woman.

The man is shaking his head, the woman, who we know to be Jennifer, the mother of Billy, has a hand over her mouth and is crying in disbelief…

Episode Eight:

Escaping Matilda (Part Three)

Jennifer Mason sat unblinking in her comfortable chair at the kitchen table, thinking. The news that her son, Billy, had been arrested for the violent murder of Doctor Striker had yet to fully sink in. Billy was a good kid. He had his faults like any teenager, but murder? Never. She couldn't ignore the fact that he had within him a dormant capacity for violence, on a scale the average person would never comprehend, but that latent evil was so well hidden, so deep within his genetic make-up, even he had no idea it was there. She unconsciously drummed her fingers on the table. Whatever she did now would have profound effects on Billy's future, she had to tread carefully. She had to… Her senses picked up something. A sulphur smell, like rotten eggs, invaded her sanctuary. She felt his presence and stiffened. The situation with Billy had now transcended bad.

'Hello, Jennifer,' he said.

'Hello, Lou,' she replied turning carefully towards him.

Lou wore a bright purple velvet smoking jacket with no shirt, and a set of yellow acrylic sweatpants, with blue double stripes down each leg. His feet bare. He ran a finger along the kitchen counter and inspected it. She stood silently waiting. It was never wise to bait Lou, you simply waited for him to reveal his intentions. He turned his head, clasped his hands behind his back and smiled at her.

'Someone's been naughty.' His snake like tongue flicked out and tasted the air.

'He's just a boy…' He was on her before she could finish. His hands around her throat, lifting her from the ground. She fought the instinct to struggle; she knew how useless that would be. Lou twisted her head this way and that, his fierce eyes burning into her. He put a twisted blackened finger against her lips.

'Are you going to beg?'

She shook her head. Meekly she said, 'No.'

He dropped her back to the ground, but kept his hand around her throat.

'You used to be so much more.' He turned from her, but his hand still held her up on tiptoes. She clung to it.

'Jennifer, Jennifer. What am I to do?'

'I'll fix it, Lou,' she croaked. The grip on her neck tightened. Her eyes bulged.

'He hit the tree,' was his reply.

'I know... that... now.' Jennifer's words came out in short bursts. Her breathing was almost cut off entirely. Again Lou turned on her.

'Grandfather Willow must be appeased.'

'No, I can fix things, please!'

He snarled at her. 'Perhaps you've forgotten who you're talking to? Perhaps I need to remind you?'

'No, Lou, please, no!'

He moved like a flash, both hands now clasped her head. His face had taken on the very depth of Hell, she squirmed in his grasp, terrified, as his eyes charged now, burning and ferocious - fire red.

'Daddy needs some sugar.' And before she could even think, his mouth was around hers, the snake like tongue pushed passed her uvula, her eyes now wide with horror, she felt it reach down into her, invade her physically and ethereally. Eventually the pulsating serpent reached into the fibre of her being, and vomit erupted from her, directly into his waiting mouth. He drank it down in ecstasy. As her breathing stopped and her brain began to starve, her eyes blackened and grew. Jennifer's skin turned leathery black and the strength of her true form burst forth. She grabbed at his head and they kissed for the longest time. Eventually Lou pulled away from her, and tossed her through the wall.

Jennifer climbed out of the rubble and stood reverently before him. Her demonic body bearing little resemblance to her human form. She lowered her eyes and dropped to a knee.

'Better.' Lou reached down and lifted her head slightly, almost gently. He pulled out a monogrammed handkerchief and wiped a small amount of vomit from off her lower lip. She did not tremble at his touch.

'He's worth saving,' she intoned, a spark of her shed humanity still controlling her.

Lou paced the room for a moment, and then looked back at her. 'Why?'

'He's my son.'

'Hmm.'

'I love him, you understand that, Lou, I know you do.'

In anger, he picked her up and punched through her chest. She screamed as her torso exploded and blood, muscle, tissue, and shit erupted around the room. He pulled out her beating heart, and then tossed what remained of her aside. She fell limply with a sickening thud and gurgled. He studied it for a moment, mesmerised by the muscles thumping in his ancient twisted hand. For a moment he was impressed by its design, its complexity. He looked back at her ruined and deformed form; she was still alive because he hadn't allowed her to die. He sighed. Bending down, he gently pushed the heart back into what had once been her chest and then he reformed her.

'Fine,' he said as he lifted her from the ground.

'Thank you, Lou.' She leaned forward and they kissed with such passion, with such visceral hunger, that it caused a shock wave of primeval, carnal lust to affect a radius of one hundred miles.

He took her over the kitchen table. The very desires of a hundred billion men could not match his sickening need, the iniquity of the world around them both, infused him, and he bathed himself in their futile hopes and dreams; their unfulfilled ambitions, their maleficent carnal desires, their unrepressed dissolute fleshly verve. Her skin boiled and her eyes burst. She reformed again and again as he continually thrust himself into her soul. He fucked Jennifer until she was nothing more than dust and then he fucked her again and again, and again. She revelled in his wickedness, his iniquitous supreme hedonistic prowess, and when he was done with her, he threw her through the kitchen counter, destroying half the house.

She looked at his back and he stepped towards what used to be the kitchen door. 'What about the murder charge?'

He stopped and turned his head. 'What murder charge?'

Again she smiled. 'Thank you.'

Lou adjusted his jacket. 'Don't fail me, Jennifer. Find a way to pacify Grandfather Willow, or I'll take Billy as I just took you.' His eyes blazed again, his desire never satiated, 'for eternity.'

She nodded, because she knew exactly what she was going to do next.

Billy sat quietly in the chair opposite the detective who had been taking his statement. His clothes still covered in Doctor Striker's blood. He had been unable to articulate the exact experience, and the detective hadn't been that interesting in hearing it. He ran his eye over the statement again and finally looked up. The scorn on his face couldn't be hidden, even if he tried – and he hadn't.

'So basically you're saying a dead girl killed him?'

Billy sighed and rubbed his face. 'Yeah. Matilda.'

'I see.' He sat back into his chair and crossed his arms. Billy went to open his mouth and say more, when the door to the room opened.

'Sarge, you got a minute?'

'Really, Foito?'

'It's about the boy.'

The detective stood and adjusted his belt. 'Don't move, kid.' He crossed the room and a conference of whispering went on. Bob finally nodded and the other disappeared. He crossed the room and picked up the papers.

'You're free to go.'

Billy just looked at him. 'I am?'

'Yeah.' The detective's demeanour had changed considerably. 'Doctor Striker died from natural causes, Lou just confirmed it.' He smiled. 'You're free to go.'

Billy continued to stare, he wasn't sure if this was some sort of game. When he didn't stand, Bob walked to the door and opened it. 'C'mon, kid, your mother is waiting.'

Billy hesitantly got up and followed him. He winced at the pain from his broken ankle.

Once he'd completed the paperwork and been handed back his belt and other personal effects, the detectives shook him his hand and wished him well. Twenty minutes later he was sitting in the passenger side seat of his mother' Pontiac. Billy had no idea what had just happened. How the hell he'd been released from the shit he'd fallen into. He felt a sense of relief he hadn't felt in a long time. Jennifer was driving; she hadn't spoken to him, other than to tell him to get in the car. He knew she was angry, but he had enough going on without trying to explain all this to her. She gave a sideways glance and he caught it. Billy just stared out the window. Eventually Jennifer pulled the car over and turned off the engine. Billy focused on her and saw a different woman in the driving seat.

'Mom?'

Jennifer considered her next words carefully. 'She'll never stop, you understand that don't you, Billy?'

He frowned. 'I don't know what you're talking about.'

She slapped him hard.

'Stop fucking lying to me!'

Billy held his cheek, his jaw loose. His mother had never so much raised her hand to him. 'What the fuck.'

She slapped him again, this time harder. It left a mark.

'Jesus Christ, Ma! Stop.'

'You hit the fucking tree, you stupid little shit.' She slapped him again. Billy held his hands up in defence. She hadn't really hurt him, just shocked him. Recovering her temper slightly she instantly felt guilty at her outburst. She reached forward and took his hands.

'I'm sorry.' His tear stained face looked up at her. She saw the anguish in his eyes and it burned into her.

'Listen, Billy. I have to tell you some things, but you can't lie to me about anything, do you understand me?'

He nodded.

She caressed his cheek. 'You are my life. I'd do anything for you, anything. I'd kill for you, you get that?'

He nodded again.

'Tell me what happened.'

He explained the story to her.

She sighed and rubbed her face.

'What the hell did I do?'

Jennifer held her mouth for a moment. 'Listen to me, Billy. I know it's going to be difficult for you to understand most of this, and God only knows, I've done my best to shield you, but there are things in this world that normal people can't see, will never be able to see. But you aren't normal, Billy, because I'm not normal.' She paused to let that sink in. He went to speak, but she put a finger to his lips. 'Let me finish. That tree you hit, we call him Grandfather Willow. He's one of the oldest demons left in this world, and you woke him up.'

'Demons?'

'Billy, the world is full of evil and that evil is channelled through millions of demons that live in it. The worst of them are locked into forms to keep them from devouring the world. There are rules, but the darkest corner of this planet has hidden in it some things that even *he* wouldn't release upon it.'

Billy looked puzzled. 'He?'

'I won't tell you his name, Billy, and I pray to a God that will never accept me, you never learn it. He is the King of all the evil in the universe.'

'You mean the Devil?'

She nodded.

'Look Billy, we have to fix this, because if we don't, I'll lose you to him.' She turned the key and put the car into drive. 'I'm already lost, but you aren't.' She smiled at him.

'What does all this mean?'

'It means I have to do some things that will save you from him, things that you aren't going to like.'

'I haven't liked much so far, and who is Matilda?'

She shuddered. 'Don't say her name aloud again. She is Grandfather Willow's protector.'

'What are you going to do?'

She looked at him hard. He noticed her eyes had turned dark, almost black. It frightened him. 'I'm going to find Harry and together we're going to sacrifice him to the tree.' Billy looked at the road in shock, trying to take it all in. Harry was his friend. Sacrifice? His heart pounded in his chest. Was this all part of the same nightmare? Was he still in bed, or in the hospital? He looked back at his mother, it looked like her, but she didn't seem anything like the woman he loved. Her face was distorted somehow. Her skin seemed mottled and translucent. He could see into her and the darkness within. And then something happened. A transformation had occurred. He looked out at the world with renewed strength that he didn't understand, yet didn't dislike either. His heart slowed in his chest. The heat from the noon sun, which usually burnt him, now seemed mildly cool. He lifted his hand out the window and held it to the light. He saw black veins pulsating through his skin. His memories, small and insignificant like a puddle, began to coalesce into a river of shared and inherited experiences. He suddenly had memories spanning thousands of years. She turned to him and he saw the demon in her.

'Good,' she said looking back at the road. 'You're tapping into your inner strength. Keep it beneath the surface, draw on it when you need too, but don't rely on it. It *will* eventually betray you to him. How's your ankle?'

'It hurts like hell. Take the next right.' His mother obeyed. 'Harry will be smoking pot at the back of Winston Park.'

They found him in the park.

Jennifer strode toward him. Billy had to jog to keep up. Her eyes grew large and blue-black, her skin began to transform and developed dark scales. Harry quickly put out the joint and stood. As she approached he saw her for the monster she was. Terrified he turned to run, but she grabbed him by the arm. He swung back to her, white faced he instinctively pulled away.

When she spoke, Billy didn't recognise the voice. It was slow and fast at the same time, like she was speaking with many voices, but all of them were her, overlapping, not quite in sync, at varying speeds. Harry's eyes glazed over.

'Don't struggle, Harry.'

He stopped struggling.

'Go to sleep.'

His eyes rolled up into his head and he fell limply into her arm.

With little effort she carried him to the car, and dropped him into the trunk. The both got back in and headed for the empty old house.

It was dark when they had finally finished tying him up. Jennifer had trussed up his feet and pulled the rope up and bound his hands behind his back. She lifted him and hung him from a low branch. She focused on her task, carefully checking the tree for signs of life. Seeing the evidence of the damage to his gigantic trunk it fuelled her. She pushed a gag into his mouth and tied it tightly around his head. Harry moaned softly, but was still out cold from the spell she'd put him under. His clothes were piled neatly on the floor. The moonlight shone on his naked body and gave him an almost bluish tint. Eventually she stepped back and Billy stood beside her.

'Is that it?' he asked not daring to look at his naked friend swinging ahead of him.

She shook her head. 'Now we have to prepare him. Billy, get my bag from the trunk.' He obeyed and came back with it. She took it from him, opened it, and pulled out a large brass bowl, a selection of bottles and an assortment of baggies and weird brass implements he didn't recognise. He dropped down beside her and watched with interest as she meticulously sorted them. When she was complete, she looked up at him.

'When did you last masturbate?'

He looked appalled. 'Mom!'

She slapped him. 'Answer me!'

Her facial aspect had changed. It scared him.

'I don't know, a few days ago maybe.'

'Take this.' She handed him the bowl.

He looked askance. 'Why?'

'Seriously, Billy. Do I need to spell it out for you?'

'No way…'

'For Christ's sake, just go behind that bush and do it! Believe me I don't like it any more than you do, but I have a ritual to finish, and that's one of the ingredients. Go! Be quick.'

'Oh, no pressure, Ma. Jesus.' He hobbled off and she feverishly continued her preparation. Within a minute he returned and handed her the bowl. She looked inside. She seemed surprised but satisfied at the volume. She placed it onto the ground beside her and began emptying baggies of something into it. He looked on disgustedly, she hadn't noticed his embarrassment. At length, she handed him a bottle.

'Drink this.'

'What is it?'

Again she flashed him a look. He put up a hand. 'Okay, okay. I'm sorry.'

'It's Ipecac. I need you to vomit into this bowl.'

She gave him another look, which suspended any further arguments. He hesitantly drank down the liquid. 'Argh, that's vile. How long does it take to work?'

'About twenty minutes.' She was grinding up some odd looking roots and sprinkling them into the bowl. He continued to watch as she made preparations. A rustling noise directed his attention back to the tree. Harry was still out cold. He watched him swing gently in the breeze. Oddly, he didn't find himself embarrassed by seeing him naked. It wasn't the first boy he'd seen that way, although it was the first teenager. His eyes travelled to the tree itself. He'd not noticed before how large it was or how far it reached across the lawn to the house beyond. He thought he saw movement. A flash of white. The air turned cold. He turned to his mother, her eyes now blue-black.

'We have to hurry.' She held out the bowl. 'Pee in here.'

'I can't pee in front of you!'

She held the bowl, her eyes blazed. Humiliated he unzipped and pointed at the bowl. He looked away and focused on emptying his bladder. It took a minute only and fresh urine splashed into the bowl she was now holding.

'That's enough.' She pulled the bowl away, and he turned and finished off to one side. He zipped up and sat back down. He didn't think things could get any worse. The night-air suddenly became arctic. He rubbed at his shoulders. Jennifer looked around her as she finalised the last of the mixture. She looked anxiously at Billy. She needed the vomit, and she thought about other possible ways of inducing him, when the emetic began to take effect. He grabbed at his stomach and groaned.

She held out the bowl. He groaned loudly and then he violently vomited, three good blasts and she pulled the bowl away. He groaned and vomited again. The pain in his stomach did not subside as his body continued to empty, even though he had nothing left to expel. He dry heaved a fifth time. Jennifer grabbed him by the head and put her mouth against his. She sucked so hard he lifted from the ground. When she was done, she simply let go. Whatever she did, it instantly took away the nastiness of the emetic and his nausea was gone. He fell back to the ground. She stood holding a brass knife.

Jennifer purposefully strode towards Harry. When she reached him, she ran the blade along his skin and drew blood. His eyes snapped open. He took in his surroundings and her, and Billy, and began to struggle. Her cuts went deeper, along his chest, down into his groin, his screams muffled by the gag. He bucked hard but he was trust up too tightly to escape. She continued cutting him, along his thigh, into his calf, along his feet. In-between each toe. His screams had become one long chorus now and as the pain and shock took control of his body, he involuntarily peed himself, as her relentless onslaught continued. The cuts were never deep enough to cause him permanent damage, they were just enough to open the veins beneath his skin and allow his blood to flow. She worked her way around him, up from his legs to his buttocks, along the small of his back and up to his shoulders. She penetrated deeper into his armpit and he cried so hard, his left eye instantly blood-shot. His sobbing agony was so extreme Billy covered his ears and closed his eyes. Jennifer continued until the only part of him that wasn't bleeding or covered with blood, was his face. When she had finished, she walked back to the bowl.

Billy looked up at her with a fearful expression. Harry was still bucking and moaning, his body covered in blood and his own urine. At some point during the horrendous ordeal, Harry had an explosive attack of diarrhoea, which was slowly running down the backs of his legs. The mixture of bodily fluids dripped unceremoniously from his toes onto the ground. Jennifer raised the knife and slit through her own wrist. Black blood poured from the wound into the bowl, and instantly the mixture began to hiss and boil. Unable to contain his own curiosity, he moved in beside her, and looked down at the obnoxious liquid. To his astonishment, he saw a million white tadpole-like creatures squirming, pulsating, and growing larger. They were consuming the vile mixture and he watched with surprise as they grew tiny mouths, and rows of sharp teeth. Their tails helped propel them inside the viscous liquid. He looked at her and frowned.

She answered his unspoken question. 'It's your sperm.'

He stepped away from her.

She brought the bowl towards Harry and stopped dead. Beside him, Matilda stood with her arms crossed. Billy instinctively stepped behind his mother.

'No! He's mine.' Matilda said, pointing at Billy.

Jennifer stared coldly at her. 'Get out of the way, Matilda, he's my son, you're not taking him.'

Matilda rushed her with incredible speed, and her visceral scream drilled into them both, but Jennifer slapped her hard and she flew into the air, and landed heavily against the tree. Matilda sat wide eyed for a moment and Jennifer took the opportunity to throw the contents of the bowl at Harry.

'No!' Matilda shouted, but it was too late. The mixture hit Harry directly on his chest. A million sperm creatures wriggled around his body. They began burrowing into the fresh cuts, eating their way into him. Harry's eyes widened at the agony of it. Whatever he had felt before was nothing in comparison. He bucked and kicked as the little creatures began eating him from the inside. Billy, Jennifer, and Matilda, now watched as Harry's body began to pulse. They witnessed large bumps underneath his skin that moved slowly. The agony and terror was almost beyond belief and yet somehow, Harry was still conscious. Matilda pouted and turned away. She reached the swing now hanging from a branch on the other side and sat in it. She held onto each rope and swayed.

They stood, mother and son, and watched as around Grandfather Willow, wisps of smoky vapours manifested into ethereal monsters. The creatures inside Harry had stopped their attack and he hung now from the low branch, listless, but alive. He could not comprehend what had happened to him, why Billy and his mother had done the things they'd done. Matilda swung slowly from her swing-seat and patiently waited. There was a creaking sound and she squealed in delight.

'Grandpa's home.'

And then the arms of the tree pulled Harry roughly into the air. He could only watch in terror as huge luminous disk-like eyes, the size of melons, opened on his ancient gnarled bark face. A massive mouth opened and a large tongue of vines flew in all directions. Harry was turned now directly in front of the gaping mouth. The branch he was on moved slowly towards row after row of sharp wooden teeth; towards slavering jaws... its lipless mouth quivered. He screamed a muffled scream once, then twice, and then jerked violently - spewing blood, muscle, sinews, and shit, in all directions as a separate branch penetrated his anus and pushed right through his body, out through his chest.

Matilda swung as hard as she could, her black hair flowing in the breeze she created.

Harry screamed no more as Grandfather Willow bit off his head, and then pulled his body apart. A millions squirming creatures slithered out of Harry's remains, towards the great tree, and penetrated his ancient bark-skin. The damage to his trunk began to heal, and he gurgled in blissful satisfaction.

And just as had happened a thousand times before, out of the darkness came an amalgam of bloated shuffling nightmarish creatures, each more horrendous than the next. They were silent, except for when they rubbed against each other, their slimy bodies slapping together, like fish in a bucket. Each of them blind, disfigured, mutilated, and dripping with grey slime. Bodies covered in bloody sores and boils that pulsated and burst releasing a spray of puss that added to their own sliminess. Ineffable ooze seeped from their rotten raw purulent flesh. Indefinable and only vaguely humanoid, they blindly pushed and pulled at each other. Their demonic senses able to detect fresh blood and entrails and they moved with hunger and speed.

The old willow laughed a dreadful gurgled laugh, as albino puss ridden horrors pawed and caressed each other. The sexual energy and latent hunger filled the air – it stank. The lasciviousness nature of their unrepressed desires sickened Jennifer and she pulled Billy back towards the car.

'It's over now, Billy. Matilda can't hurt you anymore. You're free now.'

Billy looked back at the tree and the creatures slurping on the remains of Harry and lowered his head. 'How am I not going to hell now?'

Jennifer smiled and cupped his face.

'My poor confused little man, you were always going to hell.'

Billy pulled away from her. 'Then what the fuck was all this about?'

Again she smiled at him. 'This protects you from him.' She seemed to see someone or something at the other end of the lawn, but Billy only saw the darkness. 'C'mon,' she said putting an arm around him, 'let's get the hell out of here.'

Billy looked back at his mother in a mixture of awe and disgust. Nothing would ever be the same between them, no matter how hard they tried; they'd never have the same relationship again. And as they both got into the car and drove away, Billy thought to himself – *This is going to be awesome!*

On the opposite side of the garden, against an old fashioned gaslight. Lou and Sandra stood watching.

'Well that ended better than I expected,' Sandra said, adjusting a strand of hair that had fallen into her face.

Lou nodded. 'Isn't he just magnificent?'

Sandra nodded. 'He is something, I'll grant you that.'

'The way he plunged up through his asshole and out through his chest.' Lou whistled and shook his head. 'I couldn't have done it better. He's just perfect.'

'And that's why he can't be released, Lou.'

'I know, I know.'

Sandra turned towards an alleyway that had just appeared beside them. 'You coming?'

'You go on. I need to have a chat with Matilda.'

Sandra nodded and disappeared behind a dumpster.

Lou sauntered across the lawn towards the pulsating albino monster-fest and Matilda jumped up into his arms.

'Bad man!' she said, pouting.

'Yes, yes I am.' He tweaked her nose.

'He was my play thing. Now I don't have one.' She poked out her bottom lip.

'Oh Matilda,' Lou stroked her black hair and it straightened to his touch. 'You know you can have as many as you want. But I have something even better for you.' He handed her a rabbit carcass. Its fur clumped and missing, underneath its skin maggots wriggled, their unseen movement caused it to pulsate in her hand. One of its eyes was missing. The other blinked and darted to and fro. She took it from him with glee and then hugged him tightly. She kissed him on the cheek.

'Thank you, thank you!' He dropped her down on the ground and she ran around him in circles.

'I shall call him Mr Bunny.'

And with a childish squeal of delight she disappeared off into the night.

Grandfather Willow closed his eyes and went back to sleep.

The screen displays a classic 1960s horror typographic entitled:

"Revolting Tales: Episode Nine"

The camera slow pans around a large casino. There are hundreds of players sitting at various slot machines. The camera continues to slowly move through them until it finds a roulette table.

A number of people crowd around, watching as the ball is released.

Episode Nine:

The Gamble (Part Two)

Marco farted into his cupped right hand and quickly lifted it to Miles' face, covering his entire mouth and nose. Miles pushed his hand away and made gagging noises, and then laughed.

'I still can't believe we lived through that, man!'

Marco held the door open for Miles and then quickly jumped next to him, briefly battling through the casino doors.

'Jesus, dude, it defied all odds,' Miles said.

'Let's see if our luck continues. How much cash you got?'

Marco reached into his front pocked and pulled out $120.

'That's it?' Miles bellowed.

'Fuck it; let's put it all right on the roulette table.'

'Sounds good,' Marco responded while stealing a cocktail from a passing bar maids' tray.

Marco took a sip and quickly spat it out.

'Ahhh, man this taste like fucking shit!'

'Looks like a vodka tonic to me. Let me taste it?'

Miles took a sip and followed up with a look of acceptance. 'Taste fine to me.'

He handed it back to Marco whose second sip prompted and even bigger embellishment of displeasure. 'What the fuck, dude it tastes like a combination of saline solution and someone's fucking bad taco breath.'

Miles rolled his eyes. 'Fuck it man, give me it, I'll drink it.'

They arrived at the table and solicited the attention of the oriental dealer – Miss Miling - by throwing the entire pile of cash in front of her.

She responded by counting out several $10 chips and sliding them over.

Marco gave a nasty look at an extremely heavy gentleman sitting to the left of him, sweating profusely, as he pulled the empty chair out and sat in it. He then expanded his elbows in order to make room for himself.

The man responded as quickly as a heavy man can, and moved a bit to his left. Then pulled out a very large handkerchief and mopped his brow.

'Okay Miles, you pick em, brother.'

Miles took the entire stack and put it on sixty-five.

Marco responded in a cautious tone. 'You sure you want it all on one number buddy?'

'Yeah, man, that number jumped out at me as if it was right in front of my face. Thirty-five to one odds.'

Miles sipped from his drink. He puckered as if just biting into a lemon.

'Aww, dude, you're right, this thing taste like ass.'

Marco chuckled. 'I told you, dude! And this casino smells like sweaty balls, what the fuck, over.'

Miss Miling waved her hand across the table. 'No more bet! Okay!'

She then spun the wheel and with precision flipped in the ball. All eyes were on it.

Marco suddenly reached up to his neck with his left hand as if swatting a fly.

He turned and glared at the fat man, whose attention had turned to him when he swatted the air.

Marco was sure sweaty slim-shady had reached up and touched him alongside his neck. He nudged him with his elbow.

'What the fuck, dude! Keep your fat slimy sausage fingers off my jugular, you mo....'

Just then Miles screamed out with excitement.

Marco's concentration was broken when he turned back to see they had won.

Nothing else mattered at that moment.

'Holy Jesus, Mary, and fuckin Joseph, dude, we fuckin hit it!' Miles bellowed.

They gave each other a hug and a chest bump, whilst banging the table.

'How much did we win?'

'Thirty-five to one, Marco, $4200.'

'Fuckin' A.'

A very large grossly overweight women, in a "florescent pink muumuu" of course, and sporting a perfect hairdo and nails, reached up and grabbed her lucky charms, consisting of two gnomes and a bobble-head Jesus, before they fell to the floor.

All casino eyes briefly turned to the two of them, hysterical with happiness.

And as fast as they all looked, they turned back and assumed their own pursuit of happiness and the American way.

Both Miles and Marco reached forward toward the pile of chips and simultaneously stopped, both suddenly reaching up with their right hands to rub an unexpected Charlie-horse in their necks. They momentarily stared at each other and then they just laughed.

'What are the fucking odds, huh?'

'Boy, we are getting old.' Marco shrugged and tried to twist his neck, to work out the kink, but was surprised at how stiff it had become.

Miles then grabbed a plastic bucket and filled it with their winnings. He then took a $10 chip and was about to toss it to Miss Miling, when Marco stopped him, and threw down a coupon for $1 off all you can eat Chinese buffet.

They both laughed, happy to maintain their asshole personas.

She looked at Marco and said, 'You bad. You go… fucking prick.'

Macro laughed. 'Fucking *Plick*!'

She glared for a moment, then turning to Miles, she asked, 'Are you alright?'

Miles looked puzzled. He didn't understand.

'What?'

The dealer responded once again in a slow pronounced tone.

'Can… you… hear…. me?'

Marco looked back at the fat man one last time and gave him a nasty look. He wondered if it was him that smelt like sweaty ass. He then came forward fast, with a murderous look, raising his fist, aiming a hard punch but stopping an inch from his nose. The fat man had just enough time to flinch. Marco then laughed in his fat face and turned back to where Miles was last standing. Puzzled he didn't see him.

Something on the floor caught his attention, and he quickly glanced down and saw Miles lying prostrate and stiff as a board on the floor.

'Miles!'

* * *

Paramedic Jonny Lash was grossly obese and a poor example of someone who saved lives.

He could not go an entire shift without sweating out three shirts and a pack of hefty sized tighty-whities. It was difficult for his supervisor to team him up with a crew, because no one could stand the pungent sickly sour smell that spewed from his dominantly yeast infected purulent body.

His constant flatulence caused by his poor dietary regimen of fast food and microwaved Lean Cuisine, consisting of beef burritos, tacos, and chimi chongas, could gag a maggot. His breath was so bad that it was said behind closed doors, it could knock-out a donkey at a sex show.

He poured himself out of his emergency paramedic vehicle, and hurried as fast as a heavy man could, to the pile of twisted fiberglass and metal that was once a Corvette. He was nervously excited to be one of the first at the scene. This was a rarity for a paramedic. They usually arrived after the police and fireman. He went over his training in his mind as he approached the driver's side. He let out a burp and quickly swallowed a portion of taco meat that came up with it. He then farted with each speed step he took.

He was expecting decapitation due to the roof being missing but quickly surmised it was a convertible and saw two completely intact bodies.

The driver was still strapped in. His head was bloody and leaning back against the head rest. The passenger had gone through the windshield. The upper half of his body rested to one side on what was left of the vehicles hood. He noticed a "65 miles an hour" speed sign still on its post but leaning back into the car and only inches from the passenger's face.

He could only handle one at a time and at this point his triage training told him to care for the driver.

Jonny leaned in to check for a pulse. He was startled when the driver responded by trying to push his fingers away from his neck. Jonny initially flinched, and then his surprise turned to relief knowing this guy was still alive. He began an intravenous of saline solution. As he entered the vein, he looked up to see an expression of disgust take over the driver's face. Then his expression went blank. The driver's body went limp and his breathing stopped.

'Fuck. Stay with me, dude,' Jonny murmured. He turned to reach for his oxygen and demand-valve and realised he had left it back in the van.

He had no choice but to start cardiopulmonary resuscitation. Jonny opened the driver's mouth and finger swept for any debris. He then pinched off the nose and performed a jaw lift. After one deep breath, he leaned forward and covered the driver's mouth with his. He blew in once, turned his head to one side drawing in a second breath and repeated.

To his surprise and immense relief and with the luck only a fat man with no life could have, the driver responded.

'Woooa,' he voiced thankfully.

Just then his IV tech arrived. She came forward and saw that the driver was being treated, so she moved cautiously around to the passenger side and was joined by a cute fire paramedic. They both respectively started conducting their assessments of the vehicle and passenger.

The IV tech lightly shook the passenger's shoulder.

'Are you alright?'

'Can… you… hear… me…?'

The paramedic reached over her and checked for a pulse. He then reached for his shoulder-mic and simply said, 'Code one-hundred.'

Jonny knew what was going to happen next. Hell, everyone now at the scene knew a code one-hundred meant a person with no vitals.

As the fireman positioned himself for extraction, the IV tech adjusted the stretcher. She then handed the fireman and Jonny a neck-brace each. They Velcroed the victims simultaneously.

The IV tech and fireman took hold of the passenger and quickly counted to three. They lifted and began sliding him toward the stretcher. Jonny saw that their patient's left foot was wrapped up in the seatbelt, and he quickly leaned over the driver, covering his face with a sweat soaked armpit. He unhooked the foot. The heat inside the car, coupled with his the intense concentration and bulk, made sweat drip faster onto the driver's face. Shocked into a semiconscious state he winced in frustration, pain, and disgust, turned his head to see his passenger laying on his back, stiff as a board, on a gurney.

'Miles!' he gurgled…

Devil's Cocktail!

If there is a Devil, I'm sure he loves firing up the "ol grill" and frying up a few nice pieces of fine aged Mormon or Episcopalian tenderloins, whilst sipping on a frosty blender cocktail made of.....

1. Three cocks from emaciated Nigerians.

2. One oz. of puss, from a crack whore's open and infected track wound. (Must have abscessed)

3. Seltzer with the methane of a Cambodian cow's stomach, after it lay dead in the sun for no less than 48hrs.

4. A sprits of vomit. (Anyone's will do)

5. The coagulated blood from your common cholesterol enriched, donut fed, American.

…blend to satisfied texture…

…add a garnish of toasted colon…

…and…

Enjoy!

The screen displays a classic 1960s horror typographic entitled:

"Revolting Tales: Episode Ten"

The scene opens into a familiar alleyway. The neon-sign, Caesar's Palace, flickers and is the only real source of light. As the camera pans around, we see a man enter. He pulls out a cigarette and lights it, blowing out the match with the inhaled smoke.

He paces up and down and stops as off screen, we hear the sound of footfalls...

Episode Ten:
Two raisins

Here I am, lying on my back in a fucking alley, and I think I'm dying.... Can't get up.... Can't even crawl. I got two pieces of lead in me, doing some serious damage no doubt.... Christ.... that's amazing! They can't be much larger than a raisin.... a fucking raisin! Who would have ever thought I'd be dying in an alley.... cause of death....Two raisins!

Tommy Marcik could no longer feel his arms....
Oh God! I'm really dying. This is what it must feel like!
His attention wandered, momentarily leaving behind the pain he was in. His thoughts once again dominated the reality of his situation.
Damn garbage all over the place, filth, winos, milk crates....
Cats...
Rats.
Tommy's eyes widened and again that sudden jolt of fear brought him back to his pain as he scanned the alley as best he could.
Winos!
Shit!
They'll probably take everything. My jackets, pants, boots.... Everything!
Filthy, slimy, greasy hands all over me....
Reaching into my jeans pockets like I wasn't even in them. Slobbering and drooling all over.... Burping, farting. Jesus Christ Almighty.
Farting.....ha!
A memory made him briefly smirk as a moment in time zipped through his thoughts. He was back in the diner, his wife opposite. That sour agitated face of hers she got when losing her cool, the one he loved so dearly. It always made him laugh when she exploded.
'The drooling, poppin, fartin' tart next to me!' she bellowed as they sat and had coffee and talked about her evening shift at the prison.
Somehow, all this is gonna be my fault.

His mind jerked him back…

Back to the present reality of shit… I can just see them all fighting over my wallet, ready to kill as if the five bucks in it were a million…

Aww, man! What about those fucking cats? I saw those things chew off the fingers of a passed out bum's hand. Son of a bitch wasn't even dead yet. I'll probably end up all over New Jersey in fuckin cat droppings. Christ, I'll be spread out as far as New Jer….

Holy shit! My wallet! If the bums take my wallet and the cats chew off my fingers and toes, no one's gonna know who the hell I am! I'll be just another unidentified mangled corpse to clean up. They'll scrape me up off the ground like dog shit; drop me into a plastic bag - like dog shit - then they'll take me to the morgue, dump me on a stainless steel slab, a cold son of a bitch no doubt….stick a tube up my dick….if the cats haven't chewed THAT off…. then some guy, who doesn't know me from cow dick - cows don't have dicks, dick! - Is gonna start carving me up like a side of beef.

A picture formed in Tommy's mind. He saw a medical examiner reach over him and turn on a microphone located above the stainless steel table and begin talking while placing the second of two surgical gloves on. They come down on his wrist with a snap:

'November 3, 1980, 0834 hours…. Partial corpse, tag number, seven, four, 'B' as in bravo, six, three, two, two, 'D' as in dog…. Toe tag reads at…. 1315 hours, Detective Bureau, Homicide Division, Newark, verified and cleared by this department, on this date, the undersigned, Stephen P. Sullivan, ID numbers 16-2, medical examiner.

'Initial observation as follows: Partial corpse of a Caucasian male…. Approximately twenty to twenty-five years of age… Considerable D composure due to a combination of post metamorphosis, nature, exposure to the elements, and animal cannibalism. At this time I am initiating the xiphoid process, beginning the "Y" incision now.'

Christ! Do you know what that means? He's gonna take that fucking scalpel and cut me from my fucking pituitary down to my prick!….if I still have one.

Tommy pictured a rookie cop standing behind the Medical Examiner, in a suit:

Gotta be a detective, but a rookie one by the looks of it. Figures. It's bad enough dying in an alley, raped by bums, eaten by cats, and shit out all over Newark, then butchered by the Medical Examiner. And who then investigates my cock sucking mother fucking death?

A fucking rookie!

Look…

Look at him.

Standing there with his skin turned whiter than a baby's ass. Eyes redder than a virgin's first trip. Handkerchief in one hand, covering his nose and mouth, puke tray in the other, filled twice since the Y incision…

Yeah it's "that smell" – it turns his stomach….it's like no other…. Worse than a recently methane exploded possum, hit by a car and baked out in the high-noon sun for ten hours. It's a smell that cuts off your breathing instantly. Automatic gag reflex and one you'll never forget or get used to….and of course the Medical Examiner is going to screw with him, they always do…. they love to see if they can get a guy to puke or pass out.

'Hey, officers take a look over here in the stomach cavity – we got some corn, a few clams, and um…. Oh my God, are they maggots? Have you had lunch yet, officer?'

That'll make the rookie buckle and run or the door.

Tommy jerked. Things began to come back into focus. He knew it probably wouldn't last, but he was going use the time he had to his advantage. He wanted to know what was going on around him.

More than that - to know if what he had seen and heard, prior to going down, was real or imaginary.

Was it really him?

God, the look in his eyes….

Why would he do this?….and the things he said to me.

How could he do such a thing?

Bob, of all people…

His pain began dissipating and his thoughts went to death and what awaited him after that – if anything. He was always told that just before you die, your life passes in front of you. And when the last breath leaves you, so does your soul, which slowly descends up to the heavens, a pleasant and peaceful place. He contemplated that for a second, hoping it would eventually happen. He was led to believe your whole life flashed in front of you like a recap to a movie.

Tommy was no longer sure if he was simply *thinking* things, or actually *articulating* them.

He heard a voice close to him, whispering in his ear, or inside it. It sounded familiar, yet unfamiliar at the same time. Or was it a voice inside his head? Was it his voice he was hearing? Whether it was real or imagined, Tommy knew for certain; it wasn't a nice or kind voice.

'Okay, Mr Marcik, you went and got yourself shot, eh? Just for you, we're gonna let you see a quick recap of your life and briefly let you see whatcha had, and whatcha didn't have, up until this point; and then Mr Marcik, you are simply going to die. You're not going to the place you call Heaven or the place you call Hell. You're not going anywhere. You will simply stop breathing. Your heart will stop, your brain will die, and then you will simply cease to exist. The skin will rot off your bones and eventually you will turn to dust. Dust to dust, ashes to ashes. Goodbye, Mr Marcik.'

Tommy heard the quick pitter-patter of something shuffling toward him. He had only the strength to turn his head.

A golden retriever, smaller than most, walked slowing toward him.

Hey there, little fella, whatcha doing there?

Tommy was cautious as he assessed the dogs approaching mannerisms. He wasn't sure if it was a street mutt, which would most likely try to tear off a hand or foot to snack on, or someone's pet.

The dog stood directly over Tommy looking down at him. Tommy stared for a moment again there came a sense familiarity. He knew the dog.

Jesus, you look just like my ol' dog Millie. My God, a spitting image!

He noticed a collar and a familiar town rabies-tag. (Just like the one issued where Millie and he lived many years ago.) Tommy summoned up enough energy to lift his arm in order to pet the dog, and to see if there was a name on the tag. His hand was within inches of its, no her, ear. He froze. The tag was visible and he focuses on it with astonishment. Her name was "MILLIE".

Millie bared her teeth and then, in a surreal twist, she spoke. 'I'm gonna eat you and shit you out on your mother's lawn!'

With lightning speed the she turned and bit Tommy's thumb off, swallowing it in a single gulp.

It happened so fast. He didn't have any time to react.

His scream was muted by a loud raspy voice.

'She's the same one, fucker!'

A mysterious figure approached from out of the shadows, behind a dumpster.

'That's your dog, Mr Marcik, you sick twisted fuck!'

Tommy tried focusing on the approaching man but was still dismayed at the spurting blood spewing from where his thumb used to be. He was more than dismayed at the dog feverishly licking it up as it hit the alley pavement.

He was beyond dismayed.

Since when did dogs talk?

He became further aghast when he realised several other dogs, three cats, twelve gerbils, two cut throat finches, a Hampshire ram, and countless squirrels, appeared and were all tolerating each other, while quietly taking turns licking up his blood.

Now this is one fucked up "Walt Disney" adventure.

The figure spoke again.

'Remember, dickhead? You took her out in your backyard and shot her in the head, just because she shit in the house. Then you threw her in your fuckin hillbilly fire barrel, and watched her burn while you and your dysfunctional friends chuckled.'

The voice drilled into him.

It carried on its relentless assault.

'Thought it was funny, huh? Big bad Cop. Decision maker of life and death. You and your brother holding make believe court while sitting on your deck, always finding the squirrels and chipmunks guilty before sentencing them to death by pellet gun....then just wounding them so they would lay there and suffer. You even used to walk up and piss on them you sick, cruel, fucking, fuck!'

Tommy was unable to see the figure, just make him out peripherally. He's main concern was the wildlife circling him. To say he was scared was an understatement.

'You, the keeper of civil rest, the example of good, between good and evil, the saviour of all who are in need of justice, finds enjoyment in knocking a ram out with a sledge hammer, and then cutting its testicles off. And for no other reason but to amuse the inbred, toothless, waste-of-space, fucktards, you call friends?'

Tommy tried desperately to think. Who was this guy? Despite the pain he was in, despite the fact he knew he was dying, surrounded by an ungodly amount of animals that looked all too familiar, his reply still had all the same attitude, sarcasm, and negativity people had come to expect from Tommy Marcik.

'It wasn't a sledge-hammer. It was a ballpeen hammer.'

He wanted to say more, but he simply did not have the energy. Tommy looked back at where a ram stood breathing heavy through its nostrils. He glanced down to see blood dripping from where his testicles should have been. He gazed up right into the ram's eyes and was quickly convinced it was "Scout".

Tommy used to be caretaker at "Goodert Farm" in Madison.

Mr Goodert was a retired CEO of the Bell Chandrix Corporation, and lived his remaining years as a gentleman farmer of Hampshire sheep. Tommy would care, feed, breed, and castrate the flock in lieu of free room and board.

Scout was the breeding ram and would knock Tommy on his ass every time he would turn away from him. Then, while Tommy fumbled about trying to get to his feet. Scout used to piss on him, marking his territory. Tommy hated that ram as much as the ram hated him. Scout eventually contracted tetanus after Tommy *conveniently* forgot to get him the shot, after he cut his leg on a barbed wire fence.

So when Mr Goodert asked Tommy to take Scout out the back and shoot him

Tommy said he would but actually had other plans for old Scout.

It was payback time.

'I don't think you know what's happening here, Mr Marcik.'

The figure now came into focus. There stood a man in his twenties, wearing a pair of pyjama bottoms, furry slippers, and a Metallica T-shirt. Dried vomit covered his face and the front of his shirt.

His breathing was raspy and difficult.

'Do you remember me mother fucker?'

Tommy squinted. The man did look familiar, but he couldn't connect the dots.

'Okay, I give up, help me out here pecker-head, because I don't have the time or energy to play "this is your life".'

'But that's exactly what this is, Mr Marcik. You know how you were just pondering whether or not there is a heaven or hell?

Tommy looked surprised. 'How do you know that?'

'I know everything about you, and I'm here to remind you about all the things you have most likely forgotten in that pea size brain of yours. This is your life's recap, Mr Marcik, because….you are about to die.'

The face shifted abruptly within inches of Tommy's. Gone was the puke soaked twenty-nine year old; in his place a twisted, evil, blackened, devilish visage. Tommy stared in paralysed fear along a high nose up to a haughty-brow. A black forked tongue flicked out, tasting a single tear of fear. The behemoth spoke with the sneer of an angry serpent – his words formed from thousands of different voices in unison. His eyes bore the very fires of Hell.

'He that guardeth his mouth keepeth his life; But he that openeth wide his lips shall have destruction. You can call me, Lou.'

Tommy's terror had taken complete hold of his body; he could not close his eyes.

'Look at me.' The monster's eyes engulfed him.

Unable to do anything else, Tommy stared into those black, hollow, lifeless eyes. They swallowed his thoughts, mind, and body, and sucked him into eternal vacuity. He felt as if he were flying through a still, soundless tunnel. For a brief moment, he saw his mother's face soar by. He partially heard her say in a worrisome voice,

'Oh! Tommy! What did you do…?'

And in the brief moment that followed, dazed and confused, he found himself kneeling over a cadaver. On inspection, Tommy recognised it as the twenty-nine year old man from the alley, but he was now lifeless. His eyes had the milky glazed stillness of death. The vomit on his face and T-shirt was fresh. Tommy's state of mind was frozen, paused in high-definition - and then the surroundings came alive.

Despite his initial terror, he had the presence of mind to take in the scene.

And then he remembered.

This was my very first medical call as a rookie cop.
His name was….What the fuck was his name…? Oh yeah, Bishop.
A twenty-nine year old with severe asthma…..I remember going to the call and finding him pacing around having a real hard time breathing….so difficult, he couldn't speak…..so I forced him to sit down and relax because his pacing was

getting on my nerves and making me *anxious. I didn't have an oxygen mask with me either, so I put the demand valve over his nose and mouth, turned it on high and forced it down his throat....thought it would help.*

Quick as a flash Bishop sat up and grabbed Tommy by the face.

'I was trying to tell you you're not supposed to give oxygen to a person having an asthma attack, you dumb fuck!'

Bishop then fell limply back to the floor, dead - again.

Tommy stared at Bishop's corpse defiantly, some of his earlier bravado returning. 'That's what we were taught back then.'

Tommy remembered how much he hated CPR training....actually, he hated medical calls all together. He hated the training so much he used to excuse himself to the bathroom and not come out until the written test. *Shit man, it was multiple choice. His guess was as good as any, plus the instructors were all brother officers who didn't care if you looked at your neighbours answer sheet.*

'Should have paid more attention,' he mumbled.

Bishop came alive once again, grabbing Tommy by the throat with one hand and squeezed tight enough to make him wheeze and gasp for air. He lifted him into the air, with no effort, and threw him down onto his back.

'How's it feel now, fuck face? Maybe I should show you, huh? You'd understand then, wouldn't you? Maybe you should feel it.'

Before Tommy could react, Bishop grabbed the oxygen demand valve with his free hand, turned the tank to high and shoved the disbursing end into Tommy's mouth. He then pressed the release button forcing a steady stream of pressurised oxygen down his throat. Tommy's eyes widened. Desperate to breath, and in shocking pain, his fear jumped a whole new level. He kicked and punched, but the cadaverous Bishop held him fast. He felt the strong stream of cold burning gas quickly fill his lungs until they burst, one immediately after the other. They made a sound like two water balloons striking the pavement after dropping from a ten story high-rise. He then glanced down to see with horror his stomach expanding at an incredible rate.

My God Almighty Jesus! How can I still be alive, and how the hell can I be feeling such pain without passing out?

Bishop had changed appearance again this time he looked taller, larger than life, wearing a tuxedo and bowtie. His face now an older man, with a white moustache and beard – just like Colonel Saunders. Lou laughed a gurgled laugh.

'Oh you clueless, insignificant slimy little slug. Your definition of life and all you believe is over. Your mortal reasoning and experience of pain and suffering, are minuscule now, compared to what you are about to experience - for all of eternity.'

He could only look and wait.

Lou's face had once again turned back into a fearsome demon.

The agony he endured multiplied tenfold by a single smile from the mouth of the beast. His voice, once again a union of many, spoke with lyrical harmony.

'Oh you're not waking up from this one. You're gonna feel it all. Feel the burn, maggot!"

Tommy felt the expanding pressure everywhere. The unimaginable, unfathomable, indescribable, pain of a body at bursting point, the skin stretched far beyond its own elastic tolerance. Every single nerve ending seemed to scream in outrage. Tommy screamed along with them, but at this point, his vocal-chords shredded and useless, he was unable to make any actual sound. There came a point when cotton stitching could no longer take any further stress and material ripped, the skin expanded further, internal organs began to displace, forcing spine and ribs outwards, the joints, muscles, and sinews to burst and crack, thrusting him into an entirely new level of torment.

There was a moment of stillness, a fracture of a millisecond - time seemed to actually stop. He heard the tell-tale elastic juddering, preceding an inevitable rupture, along with a muffled internal squelching.

He was going to explode….

Another billionth of a microsecond passed.

His body lifted off the ground entirely.

With a loud bang that blew out his eardrums, it finally happened. The explosion shot blood, guts, muscle, sinew, bone, and shit over everything, including Lou, who with a sickly satisfying act of desperation and hunger, began licking as much as he could from his own face. His tongue as long and green as a sea eel, the tip a hissing snake head. It could reach as high as his eyebrows. He revelled in his wantonness. The slurry was his ambrosia, his slurping tongue feverishly cleaning his hands…

Tommy felt his head drop to the floor with a dead thump and the pain of the drop added to the excruciating agony he'd just endured. He felt nauseous as he rolled with no ability to stop himself. Skin grazed and skull fractured; his nose now broken. He could compare it to motion sickness. The type one experienced from spinning round, and round, on the local fair "tilt-a-whirl".

Lou picked up Tommy's head and held it in front of him. Tommy looked into his eyes and was once again swept up into them. Moving through the black tunnel another face flew by. It was his best friend, Miles. His head rotating bodiless, his expression one of shock, dismay, pain, and horror, his mouth open and he was screaming horribly but without sound – and Tommy knew he was experiencing the same demise.

'Miles!' Tommy yelled as loudly as he could, but he was gone. The darkness and motion stopped. Tommy was back in the alley. He looked down to see his body returned, but he could not move. Lou was once again standing before him, centred amongst a menagerie of animals in various states of decay. He cradled and petted a pallid, cadaverous cat, and behind him, lost in shadows, stood several human figures.

He made a kissing noise has he bent his head down and rubbed his lips against the cats right ear. In a calm voice Lou spoke. 'How we doing so far there, Tommy boy? Still with me?'

Tommy pondered the question. When he formed an answer, he wasn't so supercilious with his response. For the first time in his miserable life, Tommy was terrified beyond words.

'Please… please let me die,' he whimpered

The horned demon-Lou again appeared inches from his face, the cat in his arms, horribly disfigured, maggots oozing from its eyes, puss from its nose, its fur and skin hanging from its mangled rotting body – hissed at him, its snakelike tongue pierced his skin. Tommy immediately recognised it as his childhood family pet, Tobias. He recalled how he and his best friend Miles got it high by "blowing shotgun" - inhaling from a pot pipe and then quickly exhaling into Tobias' mouth. Tommy remembered his delight at Tobias' useless struggle. How they would duct-tape his arms and legs together, and then throw it around like a football, leaving it taped. Or how they'd let the neighbour's dog attack it until near death. His memory was sharper than he expected. The last time he saw Tobias, Miles had taken a hit of acid and was tripping his brains out. They were in his kitchen when Tobias walked in, and for some reason, Miles become extremely paranoid and started flipping out – but instead of simply putting him outside, Tommy took "Liquid Drano" and squirted it down Tobias' throat, then threw it out the window. Miles was pleased.

Tommy's recollection brought back the devastation he felt, at the loss of Miles, who died in a car crash a few years later.

Tobias hissed again, spewing a florescent blue liquid from his mouth. It splashed and coated Tommy's face and the back of his throat. To his horror he realised it was "Liquid Drano". He choked on it. The sodium-hydroxide content burned his skin, eyes, and throat.

Lou's voice, again lyrical and thunderous, penetrated his agony.

'So, you want to die you say? Be careful what you wish for, my fine young shit coated tart of a man. You think this torment is unbearable?' His laugh rumbled like thunder - but it was more than a laugh from a single man, it was as if the entire universe was laughing at him. Eventually he stopped and his face flashed in a blur of unnatural speed to his ear. In a whisper he said, 'This is nothing, Mr Marcik. I'm being kind to you. Your depravity and unhinged deeds, your hobbies, these are worthy accolades for where you're going. Don't you understand yet? This life, this current existence, it's my playground. We have so much more to do, you and I.'

Lou's face shifted again and his voice took on a sinister cadence. 'You do not yet know what pain is, you miserable shit. Look around you. These are all the people and animals you've had a negative impact on. The ones you killed, tortured, degraded, humiliated, during their final moments in this life. Oh and don't you worry, my sick little friend, you'll remember each and every one of them as you go through eternity. I have a special place in Hell reserved for you. I've given a special waiver. I pulled out all the stops, so you could bypass several levels. You'll want to relive their final moments, but through their eyes. Just as they remembered it. Just as they felt it. Experience their pain, Mr Marcik, the final seconds of their suffering, their humiliation, horror….all of it! But you need to understand, Mr

Marcik. You have earned this special treatment. It's an honour, you do understand, don't you? You'll get all of it at once. Every notion of terror merged as one.'

Tommy tried to say something, but Lou placed a blacked finger against his lips and shushed him.

'There now, it's quite okay. There's no need to thank me…'

Lou stood and ran an eye around the ensemble. He again made a kissing noise into Tobias' ear, and lowered and dropped him with care. Tobias stood proud next to Tommy's head, still hissing, still spewing Drano.

Lou turned his back on Tommy, a huge dragon tail curled and twitched like a giant viper. He spread his hands in a gesture to the flock around him.

'You know, you've surpassed yourself, Mr Marcik. You really have. It's rare for me to meet someone as demented as you. This alley just isn't big enough to hold all the people you fucked with, over the years.' He turned and those soulless black eyes engulfed him once again. A twisted smile played across the landscape of his face. 'So I created a little surprise for you, Tommy boy.'

And just like a television VCR on fast forward, familiar faces of animals and people flew toward Tommy's face. Tommy became extremely nauseated and his eyes watered, he reached that specific moment just before one actually vomits – but then it simply stayed like it. The intensity of feeling was constant. He began to uncontrollably cry.

And with each face Tommy saw, he was suddenly inside them looking out, watching himself making snide facial expressions, hearing his own laughter, which now sounded so evil and humiliating. He saw the sickly morbid look on his own face as the 9mm pistol was pointed at him. And with each new transformation he could feel all the emotions, the pain, the suffering, of each person, every animal - every twisted action he took. He experienced the horror and terror of their last breath, whilst looking at the very last thing they saw before dying. Him!

Lou gave a head nudge, motioning to Tommy's feet. He shifted his gaze down to his bare toes. Every toenail was an actual living human or animal face. Each yelling and screaming or hissing and growling at him. A barrage of comments spewed out in unison, a cacophony of voices, their screams, their pleading – their disharmonious final moments.

You made fun of my bloating body.
I always had issues with my weight, that was no reason to eat that donut while standing over my dead body and calling me "Tons of fun".
People don't commit suicide for attention you jackass!
I was dead, you sick fuck! I can't believe you touched me like that!
You stole my engagement ring and pawned it- you low life piece of shit!
I was not just a whore, I had a family to support, ya know?

He tried to close his eyes, but Lou waggled a finger at him. His eyelids suddenly peeled off and fell to the floor. Tobias pounced on them, lumps of flesh detaching from him as he did, and he ate them up.

Tommy found himself switching between them all. Feeling everything they felt. Then just as quickly, he was back in his own body looking down at the nails on his hands, which were now the same as his toes. He focused on a dog head that was once an index fingernail; furiously it attacked a cat on his middle finger. A blur and he was now the cat, feeling the jaws of the shepherd tearing into his flesh.

Lou's thunderous laugh bellowed with satisfaction.

He leaned forward to as if to say something, then crossed his arms and raised a finger to his mouth - opened it to speak, nothing came out, and so he closed it again.

Finally, with a "clap-clap", he shouted: 'Cliché, please!'

Everything paused.

Lou clasped his hands behind his back and paced, his head down watching his cloven feet shine in the neon-light of the long since closed "Caesar's Palace". He turned to the ensemble and said, 'Smoke if you got em.'

Lou pulled out a pocket-watch from his tuxedo, which had six hands, spinning in alternative directions. He then nibbled on a fingernail and, remembering Tommy, mouthed, "Sorry" while he continued to pace. Eventually, steady footfalls could be heard approaching from the darkness. Lou smiled and raised his eyes at

Tommy, nodding. He had a childlike look of excitement on his eternal devilish face. The footsteps increased in loudness and Sandra finally appeared with her notebook ever ready. She flipped it open, went through a few pages. Lou rubbed his hands expectantly.

She finally found what she was looking for.

In monotone, she said, 'This will hurt you a lot more then it will hurt me.'

Lou jumped up and down on the stop.

Sandra turned to him. 'Did you eat your lunch?'

He rolled his eyes and gave a "sorry about this look" to Tommy. 'Yes.'

She eyed him askance. '*And* the sugared-paedophile spleens? You know how you get, Lou.'

He nodded at Tommy, still smiling, giving him the thumbs up - but out of the side of his mouth, he said: 'Sandra, I'm working!'

She snorted and closed her book.

'Working. Don't be out too late, you have an early morning appointment with Josef Mengele.'

He nodded, whilst making shooing motions.

She shuffled back into the darkness, muttering: 'I don't know why I bother.'

'I can still hear you!' He shouted back as she disappeared back into the darkness.

With a "clap-clap" he un-paused his world and the horror continued.

'And now for the grand finale!'

Lou skipped slowing toward Tommy, swayed his arms with each prance, whistling a happy tune as he did. He appeared so proud….so happy - childlike.

'Why the long face, Marcik? You're going to love this. I've spared no expense!'

He bent over and grabbed Tommy by one ankle and began dragging him toward the back of the dumpster. He continued to whistle.

"I'm so excited, Tommy. I hope you realise how special you are.' He turned his head to the crowd. 'I know you're all gonna just *love* this!"

Tommy could do nothing but look, as people and animals followed him with an orchestra of yelling, hissing, and growling. One by one they all disappeared into the shadow behind the dumpster.

Tommy was now desperately trying to keep afloat. The smell was horrifying, the taste putrid. It was hot - no it was burning. The fluid, a thickly viscous murky mustard-yellow, bubbled and boiled and pulsated. It seemed alive. Hideous figures burst forth and disappeared in froth. Shapes of people mangled beyond recognition. He had no idea where he was. He screamed as he felt something tugging at his useless legs. His strength failing, he slipped under, and then erupted back out, coughing and vomiting.

He was drowning.

Drowning…

In a river of puss.

He fought to maintain his sanity, but as he continually flashed in and out of other bodies, both human and animal, he lost track of his actions. Around him, others were in the same situation, no one acknowledged him, they were only aware of their own nightmare. Some of the people he saw he knew, others he didn't.

He saw Marco and Miles, his two childhood friends. Their bond would have kept them strong in the darkest of moments, yet here and now, they weren't evening trying to keep each other afloat – they were trying to float on top of each other.

He saw his bow hunting partner float by, desperately trying to remove two arrows lodged in both eyes. Screaming horribly in a high pitch, whilst gurgling on the puss that seeped up in to his throat.

He saw what looked like his old financial advisor, horrible mutilated and on fire, desperately trying to put himself out. It looked like he had the body of an insect – a dragonfly.

And as he spun, choked, and flailed about, he could see Lou standing along the shore, holding Tobias, surrounded by all the people he had wronged.

'Welcome to everlasting damnation, Marcik. Just one more level to go! That's when we're really gonna get started! We are gonna *partai* then, my boy!'

Lou broke out into a little Irish jig.

Humans and animals, even Scout, now all wearing party hats, blew on festive trumpets.

As Lou danced, his cloven feet kicked up sand.
All around him there were woops and cheers.
Verily they did smile.

The screen displays a classic 1960s horror typographic entitled:

"Revolting Tales: Episode Eleven"

The screen fades into a man behind a counter in a local convenience store. There are a number of people in the line for the cashier. All of a sudden the door bursts open. A man charges in shouting.

'I won!'

Episode Eleven:

The Lottery

'Hey Alison, I heard we're having you for dinner tonight?'

'Why yes you are Todd me-boy.' Alison smiled and nudged Todd with a passing elbow. In a low secretive voice Alison whispered, 'You been looking forward to this for a long time haven't you?'

Todd smiled enthusiastically, 'Oh yeah.'

Alison lightly touched his chest. 'I'll make sure I'm dressed nice and sweet, just for you.'

'Perfect,' Todd replied. Alison poked out her tongue and they departed.

Todd wiped his hands on the dish towel as he looked up at the carefully prepared serving plate, garnished with Romaine lettuce, fresh tomatoes, carrot strips, and roasted red potatoes. He busied himself making minute adjustments to the design. When he had finished, he stepped back to admire his work. It had taken some time to arrange the garnish around such a large serving plate, but now that it was done, he couldn't help but smile.

'It's a beautiful thing.'

Todd was very excited for two reasons. He had won the local lottery the week prior and his winnings were to be delivered within the hour. A nicely prepared dinner was, in his view, the appropriate way to share his winnings with friends and family. And it was amazing just how many friends and family he had. There were people coming that he hadn't spoken to in years. His excitement of the celebration increased because Alison had accepted the invitation as well. She was reluctant at first. Although she knew Todd well, they had dated years prior in high school; she was the kind of person who was very particular about this type of dinner invitation, especially if, as she had come to realise, she was to be the object of his enjoyment.

The doorbell rang.

Todd took a deep breath and then quickly walked to the door. It was impossible not to be excited about this day. He opened the door to see two smiling gentlemen in crisp white coats, holding two large colourful containers. Written on the side, in bright blue lettering: "Helvede Lottery Winnings"

'Congratulations,' they yelled simultaneously.

Todd's smile beamed at them. 'Aw, thank you, guys.' He stepped to one side adding, 'Please, come in.'

They followed Todd to the kitchen, where he moved the large serving dish of garnish from the centre island to an adjoining counter. They placed the containers in its place and then turned to him, the younger of the two looked impressively at the serving plate.

'Very nice garnish, sir, you did that yourself?'

Todd nodded. 'Yeah, was up for hours getting it just right.'

'Awesome.'

With a look from the older, the young man stepped back and they placed their hands on the handle of each container. The older man coughed slightly, then said, 'On behalf of the Helvede State National Lottery, we are honoured to present you with…' there was a slight pause and then they opened both container together, 'your winnings.'

Todd looked in and immediately let out a sigh of satisfaction. It's better than he'd imagined it would be, see the winnings, actually having them here, in his house, and not just waiting for them to arrive. Both men smiled and nodded – they loved to see the look of delight on a recipient's face. It really made their jobs worthwhile.

In one container, resting on a bed of dry-ice was the head of Alison. Her delicate mouth opened wide, stuffed with a large lemon. The other contained her skinned torso, two severed arms, and numerous organs were all vacuum wrapped and butchered to perfection.

One of the men spoke. 'We dressed her nice and sweet, as she requested.'

'Perfect,' Todd replied. He felt a tear of happiness trickle down his cheek. She was too good to him. He rubbed his hands together in anticipation.

'Well then,' the older man continued, 'you have a wonderful time sir and remember you will receive another person of your choosing, every week for life.' He handed Todd a congratulatory envelope. Todd beamed as he took it. 'Of course,' the man went on, 'the state will take the legs of each of your choices, after butchering, you know for the State General Fund and distribution to the less fortunate.'

Todd grimaced. He didn't think that was fair. After all, he paid enough taxes *and* given up his first born, he didn't believe he should have to contribute any more. But nonetheless, he really couldn't do much about it, and then he looked back into the coolers and he pushed the irritation aside. Alison really did look delicious.

'Thank you so much, guys.' Todd lifted Alison's head from the container and carefully placed her on the serving plate he had so carefully prepared.

Both men responded, 'Bon appetite, sir.'

The screen displays a classic 1960s horror typographic entitled:

"Revolting Tales: Episode Twelve"

We see a familiar casino. Groups of people are huddled around tables, playing slot machines. As the camera zoomed in to one particular table, we see large a number of people buzzing around.

Two men, we know to be Marco and Miles, are being very loud and receiving unpleasant looks from the other players around them...

Episode Twelve:

The Gamble (Part Three)

'What's wrong, Marco?'

Marco quickly spun his head around to see Miles standing next to him. His look of shock turned to confusion. 'What the...? Dude, what the fuck just happened?'

Miles frowned. 'You called my name and started yelling, *help him*, at everyone.'

'What the fuck, Miles, I saw you! You were right there,' he emphasised by pointing, 'on the fucking floor.'

Miles put his hand on Marco's shoulder.

'Hey Marco, it's okay man, calm down.' Miles smiled reassuringly. Marco was not convinced.

Miles hadn't seen Marco this agitated about anything before. He could tell that his friend had truly freaked out.

Miles publicly adjusted himself and scowled at the table attendant. 'That fucked up drink....must have had something in it.'

This explanation made sense to Marco, it made a lot of sense. 'Yeah, something like that....someone probably slipped in a "Mickey".' He closed his eyes in an attempt to shrug off the uneasy feeling in his mind. Miles was staring at him with his best pretence at looking concerned. It made Marco smile. 'It's Okay.'

Miles' eyes lit up. 'Come on!' He belted out, playfully punching him. 'Think of the money, brotha!'

Miles held the cash up, waving it provocatively. 'Huh...?'

Marco's confusion and self-doubt melted instantly, a smile slowly crept across his face. 'Yeah, Baby!' he yelled over the crowd.

The both walked quickly through the crowds, pushing through people without a care. Miles deliberately knocked into a smart well-dressed older woman – clearly trying to appear twenty years younger. She dropped her notepad. Miles stopped and they made eye contact.

'Oh, I'm sorry. Here, let me get that for you.' He bent down and picked it up and handed it to her. She reached for it and as she made tactile contact, Miles pulled it away and threw it over his should. She tilted her head and looked deeply into his eyes. Miles leaned in menacingly. She matched his look, saying nothing. Miles leaned right into her face, their noses almost touching, and laughed loudly in her face. She made no reaction at all. Her expression was simply unreadable. He turned and still chuckling, jogged to catch up with Marco.

Her eyes followed him, as he swaggered next to Marco. She clucked her tongue in that school mistress way and with a snap of her fingers, the pad instantly flew to her waiting grasp. She tapped it lightly to her face for a moment; her narrowed eyes never left him. Eventually she opened it, pulled one of the many pencils that kept her grey-hair in a perfect bun, and made a few notes.

Marco looked over his should as Miles approached.

'Dude, did you see that stupid old hag. I totally owned her.'

A short Texan walked past, puffing on a huge cigar. In a swift movement, Marco pulled it from his mouth, and pushed him away. His protests squashed by the menacing advance of Miles. He growled and turned tail.

'Come on, Miles.' Marco puffed furiously. 'Let's get a room.'

They both arrived at the reception. A striking blonde receptionist smiled at them.

'Welcome to the Casino Hotel. How can I assist you?'

Marco checked out her name badge and her cleavage. Her name was Mary.

In what he thought was his sexiest tone, Marco loudly asked, 'How much for a room, sweet-tits?'

Mary smiled an oh-so-practised plastic smile. He dumped his casino card on the table and she picked it up, swiping it through the card-reader. Her screen showed his details. She looked up.

'Oh! Congratulations, Mr. Bovolocca. I see you were lucky this evening.'

'You could get lucky too, *Mary*.' The cigar waggled between his teeth as he spoke. Marco grabbed his crotch and raised his eyebrows.

Mary's smile never broke. 'The house would like to "comp" you a room.'

They looked at each other and cheered, chanting, *'Yeah! Hootie hoot hoot, let's do some toot!'*

Mary suppressed a grimace and handed them registration cards. Miles started filling them out, while Marco strolled to the reception couch to scope out the chicks.

Mary, smiling sweetly, busied herself on the computer.

Miles glanced up at her.

Mary, nice easy name to forget in the morning.

She was cute. He was going to ask her up to the room to do some blow, but she didn't look up. She reached for the paperwork and looked up as another receptionist hurriedly walked passed saying: 'Activate crash-cart please, ready room G8 ....code blue.'

Mary handed Miles the keys to their room. He stuffed them into his shirt pocket.

Miles looked puzzled for a moment. Mary had disappeared. He craned his neck to see around the reception wall to the room beyond, but the door was closed. He shook his head. He heard it wrong, that was it. *She probably said something like activate key-card for room G8, the blue coloured one.* Miles always found ways to rationalise the things he hadn't heard correctly. He was confident she would eventually come back; he was even more confident that she would look at him in "that way", eventually he would take her to bed. He turned to see what Marco was doing. He slowly scanned the lobby and quick movement caught his eye.

His vision blurred a little. He stood quickly and instantly felt nauseous, dizzy. His vision tunnelled. Marco was lying on the lobby couch flailing uncontrollably. There were two people standing over him. One was holding him down by the shoulders while the other was trying to tie his hands to the couch arm rails. Miles lunged to his best friend's aid but he was stuck fast. His legs would not cooperate with his need to be at Marco's side. He turned his head as a noise alerted him. Mary had appeared very close and was looking directly into his eyes whilst holding a very large pair of scissors.

'Call security!' Miles yelled at her.

Mary snipped the air with the scissors seemingly ignoring his hysterical call for help. 'Now, now, you and your friend are perfectly fine, sir, you need to hold still for me.'

Miles franticly turned back to check on Miles, and his legs suddenly worked. He lurched forward and ran right into Marco, who grabbed him by the shoulders.

'Whoa dude! Where you off to?'

Miles stared at him for several seconds. Trying to remember who he was. He quickly looked around in all directions.

Nothing was happening.

Everyone was simply going about their business as normal.

Miles turned back to reception.

Mary was casually typing something into the computer.

He was totally disorientated.

Marco shook Miles hard. 'Dude, you seeing things too?'

Miles looked back at him but was still processing his surroundings and could not talk.

Eventually Marco laughed and released him. 'It must have been that fuckin' drink man! Fuck it, let's enjoy the high! Come on, let's go!'

Marco pulled Miles by the arm toward the elevators.

***

'Code blue, ready crash cart!'

The emergency room supervisor, Doctor Gareth Winslow, ordered in a calm yet demanding voice. 'I need 3 ccs of Epinephrine, readied stat!' Winslow looked to her side. 'Julie, could you ready him please.'

Emergency room nurse Julie Banger grabbed a pair of scissors and started cutting the laces off Marco's right shoe. With care and training, she eventually cut all his clothes off, carefully bagging them, and began to conduct a complete and full body assessment, to look for further injuries.

'Mary, can you do the same for the passenger please.'

Nurse Mary was the alternate emergency nurse called in to assist. She grabbed another pair of scissors and approached the passenger on the adjoining gurney.

As she approached, Miles became momentarily conscious and started to flail around. Mary spoke to him in a calm reassuring tone.

'Now, now, you and your friend are perfectly fine, sir, you need to hold still for me.'

She started cutting his shoe laces off. Miles turned to see Marco on the gurney next to him. Doctor Winslow and Julie were strapping his hands down. They injected 3ccs of Epinephrine directly into his heart. It took only seconds for Marco to react.

Both Miles and Marco lay side by side restrained in the ER.

While the doctors and nurses looked and assessed the scans and charts, Doctor Winslow's worry was not the trauma to their bodies, even though they were both in bad shape, would require extensive surgeries and months of rehab. His primary concern right now was the swelling of their brains, caused by the blunt force trauma.

Just then Marco spoke - and it made no sense. However, a spontaneous utterance was common with brain trauma patients, so everyone glanced for a moment before turning their attention back to whatever they were doing.

'Hootie, hoot, hoot, let's do some toot.'

Doctor Winslow's prognosis was that it would be an extremely tough night for them both. He wasn't a betting man, his experience, and the charts and medical facts before him, showed very clearly that there was a high probability they would not survive the night. He discussed the facts with a fellow doctor, who nodded in agreement. To help increase their odds, Doctor Winslow put them in a chemical induced coma.

It was touch and go, intensive care nurses worked alongside Mary and Julie. They were prepped for the night and then in unison, they unlocked both gurneys and pushed them to the elevator. As they approach and the doors opened, alarms monitors rang, Miles and Marco had flat-lined. They frantically worked on them in front of the opening and closing elevator doors for thirty minutes, along with Doctor Winslow. He eventually called it at 10:22. He left them and picked up his paperwork. At the desk, he dialled the morgue.

'Lou? This is Doctor Winslow. We have two for collection. Emergency room. Yeah, better get help, unless you can manage two on your own? Okay, Mary and Julie are with them now. Thanks, Lou.'

* * *

'Let's check out the room and find some blow,' Marco said excitingly. Both reached for the elevator button at the same time and jokingly did the reach in slow motion. They were inches from the button, when the casino recess ceiling lights blew in sequence. Six in all. They went off like muffled shotguns. Miles and Marco covered their heads with their arms in order to protect themselves from the falling filaments.

'What the f….' Marco bellowed.

Miles grabbed at Marco. 'You alright, buddy?'

'Yeah, yeah, I'm okay. Jesus Christ, what else can fuckin' happen today, my God.'

The elevator door opened and there stood an attendant dressed so shockingly, both Miles and Marco had to exchange a quick look before stepping forward. To say he was overdressed was an understatement. Dressed to kill would suit him better. He stood rigid, his gold suit with dark red trim contrasted horribly with the pink sequinned waistcoat and neon-orange shirt. His black bowtie matched his patent leather shoes – and his "bell-boy" hat, perched to one side from his enormous head. His shoes sparkled so brightly it dazzled them, and they both shielded their eyes as they approached. He stepped aside as they entered. For the first time since they'd walked into the casino, they had no comment.

The attendant asked, 'What floor, gentlemen?'

Marco's thoughts were still preoccupied by the exploding lights. He tapped the attendant on the shoulder. 'Did you fuckin see that dude?'

The attendant simply chuckled, and then repeated his question.

'Floor, sir?'

Both Miles and Marco gingerly swiped at each other's shoulders, brushing off broken glass and filaments. The attendant patiently waited.

Miles shook his hair out. 'We're going up to the sixth floor.'

Marco felt fragments of glass deep in his scalp and winced. 'What the hell, man.' Carefully removing another fragment he and Miles were not paying much attention to anything other than their own discomfort. They didn't notice the smile playing across the attendant's face. Didn't notice the way his eyes blinked vertically, took no notice that his shoes had somehow disappeared and were now replaced with large cloven feet.

Lou pressed a bright red button on the panel.

'Down it is.'

Marco and Miles were too shaken and concerned with their own issues to pay any attention to some bizarrely dressed freak; they therefore didn't hear what he had said. The elevator doors shut instantly – and then two things happened. Firstly, the elevator dropped so suddenly, Marco and Miles found themselves pinned to the wall and ceiling. The force was so extreme they couldn't do much more than fight to stay in one place. Marco was flipped upside-down, his feet on the ceiling and his head pointing to the floor. In contrast, Miles was head uppermost. Secondly, the elevator started playing generically composed music so loudly their screams were drowned by it.

Lou stood comfortably with his hands clasped behind his back as the two of them tried desperately to right fight against the force. The elevator music seemed to increase in volume, as Lou gently began tapping his foot to the melody. His body swayed gently, as the music took him. Eventually he started to torso dance – his hands in fists rhythmically bouncing left, then right, his head bobbing as the speaker blasted the pan-pipe version of an old Eddie Money song. He looked up at the two men pinned to the elevator walls. They were voicelessly screaming. He smiled at them both.

He closed his eyes and began to sing.

'I'm gonna take you on a trip so far from here, I've got, two tickets to paradise. Won't you pack your bags, we'll leave tonight.' He gave them the thumbs up as he continued his off key warbling. 'Two tickets to paradise… Isn't this great?' He beamed and continued to dance as if he was squashed up against a group of people and was trying not to touch them.

'We're gonna die!' Marco screamed. Miles' scream echoed his sentiments.

Lou's face changed. His eyes became so large they seemed to fill the elevator. He reached up with the speed of a striking cobra and pulled their two heads together so fast, neither had a chance to react. In the voice they betrayed his iniquitous nature, the unison of millions, he bellowed: 'You're already dead, you insignificant lowlife pieces of snail shit.'

Lou's snake like tongue burst from his blackened mouth, and took a bite out of each of their faces. Their screams continued as he pushed them back to their relative places on the ceiling and walls. They continue to shriek and yell and Lou's malevolent laugh filled the space between. He jumped up and mimicked them both, grabbing his head and screaming with such pitch the glass in the button panel shattered.

'Two tickets to paradise, Baby! '

Smoke began to fill the enclosed room, and Lou found the look of horror and panic on both their faces, gorgeous. The smoke began to solidify, forming grotesquely deformed hands and arms of all shapes and sizes. They seemed to merge out of the walls, and with them, so that they formed part of the elevator itself. Marco squealed and tried unsuccessfully to squirm out of reach, as arms began to grab him. Fingers took hold of clothing and skin; they curled around his thighs, and his throat, then around his chest, and finally locking him against the wall the last of them around his midsection. The same ethereal hands quickly manifested around Miles and his struggled too, was futile. Faces began to push their way out of the walls. Twisted, half formed and – at first – unfamiliar. Mile and Marco had hands across their mouths now, and as the faces formed features, they both began to recognise them. These were the faces of people they had betrayed, cheated, abused, ridiculed, and maligned.

A white flash so bright filled the room and Miles found himself in bed.

He blinked a number of times at a ceiling he didn't recognise. He looked down at his naked body, saw the girl sitting beside him, also naked. He dropped back into the pillow and rubbed at his eyes. He sighed in relief. It had been a dream. A fucking dream. He looked up at her, and she back at him. She ran a finger along his chest and he felt his dick twitch. Despite the horror of the nightmare, he was instantly pulled back in the real world. Some whore was about to blow him, and he smiled. It was Mary, the receptionist. He recognised her instantly.

Miles shook his head. 'You would not believe the dream I just had...'

'You have a very nice dick, Miles,' she said, running a manicured fingernail along its growing length. He shuddered at her touch.

'It's all yours, baby,' he said, interlocking his fingers and resting his head on them, into the pillow. She flashed him a smile.

'Really? Mine?'

'Yeah, do what you want, baby, he's all yours.'

'Him? You named him?'

Miles shrugged. 'I named him Bob, now blow me.'

'Hello, Bob.'

Miles rolled his eyes. Mary looked back at him. 'Thank you, Miles, he's beautiful.'

He quickly tired of the nicety. He thought about what Marco might say at that moment. Eventually he said, 'Whatever, Mary, just suck me the fuck off, Jesus.'

She leaned forward and lightly kissed his frenulum.

He sighed. *Finally.*

She placed her left hand on his chest and he closed his eyes as he felt her carefully take hold of him. Instead of the anticipated warmth of her mouth, he felt a sharp pressure on his chest. It instantly alarmed him. He looked up in shock as his body was being pushed into the bed - hard. He felt a sharp pain as something cracked. She didn't appear to notice his alarm. The pain in his chest was so terrible, it took his breath away.

'Jesus, Mary!'

She had pinned him to the bed and panic began to settle in. He grabbed at her arm, but couldn't release it. He tried to punch at her face, but it was out of reach, so he settled for her arm. She still held him down, and in her other hand, she held his member tightly. He looked down as she began to stretch it. He looked back at her, but again she didn't seem to notice, or care, that he was struggling against her. He desperately tried to remove her arm, but despite his best efforts, he couldn't. And it was then that Miles realised what she was about to do. His eyes opened wide at the horror of it.

'No, no, stop… please, please, please… no…'

Ignoring his attempts to break her hold, she looked at the penis she held tightly in her right hand.

'I think I'll take you home with me, Bob.'

'No, no, please… no… Mary…'

And with a violent jerk that made Miles shriek so hard, blood sprayed from his torn throat - the trauma so intense and unexpected, he vomited across his chest and over her hand - Mary pulled his penis and testicles completely free of his body. Skin split, blood spurted from the severed and exposed Corpa Cavernosa and she lifted her prize proudly into the air. Seminal vesicles and an assortment of blood vessels dangled, oozing blood and fluids, along with half his bladder and other unrecognizable parts of his urinary tract – and all the time, she effortlessly pinned him down. Placing her trophy onto the bed, she reached into the cavity and dug deeply inside. Miles twitched involuntarily in mental detachment, his traumatised mind unable to process much of what his eyes were seeing – as if the synapses had been overloaded and were no longer accepting rudimentary data. He felt her pushing, pulling, pawing at his insides – it no longer hurt - eventually she pulled out what he knew to be his prostate, and she bit down through the fibromuscular tissue. Under the pressure, fluid within burst out and seeped down her chin. She closed her eyes as she swallowed it, her fingers wiping fluid from her chin back into her mouth.

'Mmmm, so sweet.' She licked and sucked each finger dry, and when she was done, she lifted Bob and sighed in satisfaction.

Miles babbled incoherently as he violently shook. Devastation had now taken the place of pain and he stared at what remained of his penis, hanging from her blood smeared hand. He cried at the injustice of it, at his impotence, at his inability to stop her, and in rage and wretchedness he screamed again, and again, until there was no air left within him to continue. She turned, holding it up in front of his horror struck face - he cried harder.

'He's beautiful. I love him. Thank you.'

'You fucking bitch…' he managed to voice through woeful sobs. 'You fucking bitch!'

She carefully laid it down beside his bucking body and released his chest. He took in a deep breath; the pain from his cracked ribs almost overwhelmed him. With what little strength he had, he reached for her, but she knocked his hands aside and pushed him back onto the bed.

'Shhhh, there, there, Miles, baby.' He tried to sit up again, she pushed him back down. Eventually the shock coupled with hypovolemia, and the realisation that he would never be able to have sex with anyone ever again, crashed him back into the pillow.

'You fucking bitch…' Tears rolled sideways from both eyes, down pallid cheeks.

She took his head gently between two hands and looked directly into his eyes. He spat vestiges of vomit in her face. Ignoring it, she simply leant forward and kissed him gentle on the forehead. He cried out at her touch and before he could react, or respond, her hands twisted, sharply. The last thing Miles heard was the sickening grinding, popping sound of his neck snapping.

Moments later, he awoke, screaming, back in the elevator.

Lou was still singing when Miles' eyes snapped open.

'Welcome back, Miles!' he shouted. 'Your ticket to paradise is almost printed!'

Marco was disorientated. He tried to sit up but found his body unresponsive. The light was dim but he was able to see around him, just. At first he thought he might be paralysed, but then he saw he was simply restrained. He pulled and twisted but was unable to break himself free from the bonds that held him firmly on what appeared to be some form of table. A spot light suddenly shone brightly into his eyes and he closed them tightly in surprise. When he opened them, he found he could see a lot more of the room. It was some kind of studio. There were cameras and autocues. There didn't appear to be anyone manning them.

'Hello?'

Silence.

'Is there anyone there? What the fuck! Why am I tied to a fucking table, you sick mother-fuckers.'

There was a whoosh and then a voice shouted, 'Ta-da!'

The unexpected vocalisation, followed by a multitude of brightly coloured lights and a fanfare from an unseen band, to his right, made him jump. He turned his head, and there was the oddly dressed elevator attendant. He now had a bright silver suit, with no shirt this time. He heard a murmuring to his left, and where there was originally darkness, now sat row after row of audience. He couldn't make them all out, but many of them, sitting in the front row, were people he recognised, people he knew, or people he'd known. Fat obese men and woman he'd ridiculed, hookers he'd fucked and cheated, animals he'd maimed or had used for sexual gratification, family members he'd lied to, defrauded, tortured, raped. All in various stages of decomposition, and all seemly excited.

The host leaned down.

'Welcome, Marco!' he bellowed.

The audience began to clap.

'Where the fuck am I?'

Lou smiled. 'You're on the set of my new show, *Wheel of Misfortune*. You've done so well up to this point,' he turned to the audience. 'Didn't he do well?'

A chorus of "yes" and laughter.

Lou beamed. 'You're now at the bonus round.' A small wheel appeared beside him. He spun it, and when it stopped he picked up an envelope.

There is a rousing sound of applause from an audience.

'Well let's just see what your prize is, shall we?'
Marco tried to free himself violently. The restraints tightened and he noted with horror, that they were snakes.
Lou carefully opened the envelope and pulled it out. 'Oh! Now this is a great prize, Marco. You actually get a choice.'

The audience make "ooh" sounds

Marco sneered. 'Let me go, that's my choice, fucker.'
Lou waggled a finger.
'No, no. You have to play the game. Here are the rules. I'm going to give you the choice of two fabulous prizes, and you have to pick one. If you don't, I get to spin the wheel again and whatever is in the second envelope will be your choice. Understand?'
'Whatever.'
'Excellent. Are you ready? Then let's play...'

The audience shouts: "The Wheel of Misfortune".

'Okay, Marco, here are your choices. Number One: Death by chocolate.' He leant forward and whispered, 'I have to say this isn't my favourite.' He then stood back and bellowed, 'Number Two, oh this one is great, death by liquefaction. You have to pick one.'
'Fuck you. I ain't playing your sick game, whoever you are.'
Lou pouted. 'Well you know what that means.'

The audience shouts: "Spin the Wheel!"

Lou spun the wheel hard, and Marco began to sweat under the lights in the studio. He eyed the snakes holding his arms and legs in place. Eventually the wheel stopped and Lou picked up an envelope.

'Oh well, Marco, you probably should have gone with one of the other choices, this one doesn't have the feel of a good prize.'

The audience makes "aww" sounds.

Marco definitely met Lou's gaze but said nothing. Lou raised his eyebrows a few times, whilst he slowly, carefully, opened it and then he looked over at Marco with a surprised look on his face. 'I take that back, Marco my boy, this one is fantastic. Real old school.'

The audience repeated "Old School."

Marco just stared at him.

'Well Marco, you have won….' Marco heard a drumroll as Lou excitedly held the envelope to his face. 'Death by Logging-Saw.'

The audience whoops with delight and breaks out into rapturous applause.

Another spotlight snapped on, and to Marco's horror, he could see the end of the table. Positioned in the centre, he could just make out the leading edge of a huge saw blade. It instantly spun into motion and the table jerked and shuddered as it slowly moved towards it. Marco, wide eyed, began hysterically fighting the bonds that held him. The uselessness of his task escaped him and as the table slowly moved forward. He turned to Lou, who was walking slowly beside him.

'Dude, let me go, please.'

Lou shook his head sadly. 'I'm sorry, "dude", you didn't pick one. That was the rule. This is it, Marco. You had your choice. Just like your choices in life.' He pointed to the audience. 'You recognise them don't you?' Lou didn't need an answer to know the truth of it, he knew everything. 'So that was that, Marco. You started off a blank slate, had the chance to be a good boy. If you'd stuck with that, well... things would probably have panned out okay, but boringly. Or, be the bad boy. Now we get to play with each other for eternity.' He smiled. 'You see Jenny over there?' Lou waved; she stood and jumped up and down on the spot, frantic and hysterically happy at being noticed, to be singled out. She waved both hands at him and Lou laughed.

'You remember Jenny, don't you?'

Marco watched her bounce as Lou continued to talk.

He knew her.

'Now there was a nice girl, she didn't mess with anyone. But you changed that didn't you, my boy? Slipped her something into her drink, then you fucked her until her innocence was destroyed. Did it end there? No. That's what I like about you, Marco. You were there to comfort her when she came around. You were the strong arm that kept her going, she had no idea it was you, and you loved every minute of it... Oh how you did it again and again, but she being so naive –' He waved to her again.

'She, who had no idea you were raping her continually and living off the money you raised, the campaign you spearheaded in her honour, in her defence. Oh... it was inspired, truly. Then you did what any of us would do when you got bored of it, 'cause let's face it, there's only so many time you can do it before it gets boring right? You drugged her, dropped her into the bath, and watched her drown. Totally understandable. It gave you a *hardon* though, didn't it? Marco, I'm *so* glad you didn't follow that sickening regime of goodness.'

Marco never took his eyes off the attendant. 'How the fuck can you know all this shit?'

Lou leaned in.

'I am the original cherub, the anointed who covers. The very highest of all His creations, Marco.' And for an instant, in his mind only, Marco was given a tiny glimpse of the man whom he saw beside him, a man no longer. Standing eighteen-feet tall, every inch of his body covered in eyes. His cloven feet splayed at his weight and his four-wings flexed over eight feet, also covered in eyes. Lou, the father of lies, turned his four faces - cherub, man, eagle, and lion – and laughed maniacally as the very fires of hell and all that was unfathomable filled the tiny human mind – and Marco cried and burned at the very knowledge of it.

And then he was simply Lou.

'People always say to me, hey Lou, how did you know? How could you know?' He moved with such speed and filled Marco's entire face with two pulsing black eyes. 'I'm the keeper of all that is hellish in design in the universe. You think I won this job in a fucking raffle?'

Marco shook with fear.

'Hey Marco, what was Jenny's favourite game show?'

'Wheel of Fortune.' He whispered.

'Oh! Look,' Lou pointed. 'The saw's about to bite.'

Marco looked down as the table he was bonded too began to shudder violently. The Saw had started cutting slowly through it, and was now in-between his ankles. Lou leaned forward so that he could see directly down Marco's body, and the path the blade would follow. Marco's bravado had abandoned him. Sweat was pouring furiously from his pours. Lou pinched at his nose.

'Pew, someone's stinky!'

Marco watched helplessly as the blade had moved along the middle of the table, just passed his knees.

'For Christ sake!' He shouted. 'Someone help me!'

Lou laughed.

'Funny you should mention Him.' He again appeared beside Marco's right ear, 'Wanna know something funny?' He leaned in and whispered into Marco's ear.

Marco wasn't paying any attention. 'Help me! For god sake, please!' The intensity of Marco's fear had deadened his senses. Whatever it was that Lou just whispered about Christ in his ear was lost as the blade had just reached his crotch. The fibres of his Levi fly began to fray as the blade slowly cut through and hit the zipper.

'Help me! Help me! Help me! For g… Arrghhh!'

Lou scrunched his entire body up and bit at his lower lip in anticipation, and as Marco began to scream, and the intensity of those screams grew in urgency and volume, he turned towards the audience and smiled broadly – looking directly at Jenny and gave her a big thumbs up. She squealed in delight. Marco's screams turned from panic and fear to gurgled agony. And Lou sighed in a satisfaction that made him shine in the darkness.

'There's nothing quite like the sound of a man being slowly sawn through, groin first.'

The audience began to clap.

Marco screamed and screamed and screamed as blood, muscle, sinew, tissue, bone, and shit, sprayed across his face and halfway across the stage.

The audience clapped harder. They began a slow chant in unison as the blade ploughed through his pelvis.

His Intestines ripped and flew along with anything caught in the teeth of the blade. His diaphragm and his stomach - which had emptied itself already - burst and sprayed its acid along with everything else.

The audience's chanting picked up speed as the blade began to saw through Marco's ribs.

Lou leaned over and licked at Marco's face. His agony was beyond his ability to actually reason it. Yet he felt everything, every cut, every burst organ, every nerve being ripped and pulled. His spine cut through, the vibration as the blade hit his sternum. How Marco was still alive he couldn't fathom. The blade severed his heart and Lou grabbed at the half that was exposed and began eating it.

The audience's chanting became faster and faster.

The blade was about to cut through Marco's chin and then it was over. Marco completely in half. His eye movement on each half frantic. He was able to see the audience and Lou at the same time. He couldn't speak but he could feel everything. It was nightmarish; beyond reason, beyond sanity, an immeasurably, incalculable, horrifyingly incongruous experience.

And when Lou had finished eating the last remnants of the heart, he wiped his mouth and said: 'Ready for round two?'

Marco jolted awake and found himself back in the elevator.

'Welcome back, Marco! Your tickets to paradise will soon be ready, so enjoy the ride boys!'

The elevator continued to drop, Macro and Miles, their faces covered by hands, could see nothing and say nothing. Neither could understand what was happening to them, and as the pressure of the fall continued, they were for a moment only, able to look directly into each other's eyes. Neither one of them was particularly comforted by what they found there.

There was a screeching sound and Lou smiled. 'Wait's nearly over boys.'

The door opened and silhouetted in the doorway stood Sandra. She walked in carrying an envelope in one hand and a brown paper bag in the other. When she was fully inside, the doors silently closed.

Sandra walked forward with purpose. She looked up at Miles and smirked. He recognised her from the casino. She handed Lou the envelope. When Sandra saw Mile's realisation had sunk in, she pulled a pencil out from her hair, walked up to him and without pause, pushed it into his right eye.

Lou cackled: 'Oh! That's gonna leave a mark!'

Sandra pulled out her pencil and pushed it back into her hair. Miles was still screaming, his right eye was now hanging loosely from its socket.

'What's in the envelope?' Lou asked.

Sandra sang, 'Two tickets to paradise.'

Lou held it close to his chest. 'And the bag?'

'Lunch. You forgot it, again.'

'What would I do with out you, Sandra?'

'I shudder to think.' She handed him the bag. 'Just a quick reminder, you have an eight fifteen with Gabe. You know how grumpy he gets when you're late.'

Lou was peering into the bag. 'Oh! Jellied Taliban Babies. Seriously, they're my favourite.'

'I know.' She reached up and pinched his cheek, then turned and left.

The elevator suddenly dropped again and the pressure was more extreme than ever. Lou reached up and carefully pushed Mile's eye back into his socket. The elevator began to spin and the nebulous hands released the two men. They began free falling. They crashed into every part of the small room. Their shouts in unison. And Lou simply stood there, hands clasped firmly behind his back. The room stopped spinning, and continued to fall. Both men were held in place again by the wall hands, and now they were facing each other. Miles above, Marco below.

Miles, unable to take any more, vomited violently right into Marco's mouth; the force of his vomiting caused both his eyes to pop from their sockets, dangling downwards. The hands that held them also held their mouths open. Neither could move nor fight. Marco tried in vain to turn his head as more vomit poured in.

Not a drop missed its mark.

Marco was almost drowning in vomit.

The elevator came to a sudden stop and the hands released. Both men fell to the floor hard.

'Your floor, gentleman,' Lou said stepping aside and gesturing to the bright yellow light streaming in through the doors. 'Your suite awaits you.'

He opened the envelope and pulled out the two tickets. He put one in their shirts.

They both just lay on the floor. Unable to move, unable to speak. They were too terrified to do anything. Miles couldn't even raise his arms to fix his dangling eyes. Eventually Marco stirred. He pushed himself upright. He had dug deep into himself, and gathered some form of composure. He held out a hand to Miles who shakily held onto it. Marco staggered forward and looked outside the doors and he sighed. He pulled Miles beside him. Miles was trying to push one of his eyes back in but Marco stopped him

'You don't wanna see this dude.'

'Wha... what's... out there?'

Marco stood staring at the scene before him. 'Well. It's a river or sea, or something.'

Miles, shivering said, 'That doesn't sound so bad.'

The stench of the putrid liquid wafted in through the doors, both men held their noses.

'What the fuck is that smell?' Miles gagged.

'It's the river, dude. It's kinda yellow, well, maybe brown, mustard colour.' He sighed. 'It looks like puss dude.'

Lou put a hand on both their shoulders. 'C'mon, boys, so many people are *dying* to meet you.' He gently pushed at them and they staggered forward into the bright light and soft sand. Marco looked back at Lou.

'This is hell, right?'

Lou pinched his cheek. 'Not quite, Kiddo. This is a waiting area, but I like the way you're thinking. Think of this as a vacation spot, a place for you both to relax. Have fun, enjoy the scenery, prepare yourself, you know what I mean.'

'Seriously?' Marco brightened.

Lou looked serious for a moment, then his composure broke and he laughed. 'No, not really.'

And he picked them both up by their necks, lifted them up and with the grace of a professional footballer, kicked them high into the air.

They flailed and in slow motion they fell, and they fell. Arrows flew at them, hit them, pierced their skins. Miles screamed as they continued to fall. Casino chips and rolled up balls of toilet paper peppered them both. Huge creatures, dragonfly like, swooped around them, bathing them in fire. In the distance, Marco could see the source of the river. A large volcano was erupting, pimple like – no an actual pimple - its puss-lava slipping down each side, slowing as it solidified. The thickly vicious liquid above formed a crust, and beneath it flowed fast, feeding into the river they were falling into. The horizon was full of them. Pustules and boils as far as the eye could see. Foul smelling, abscessed and putrid, red and swollen, the heads bright white and rhythmically pulsating. Macro watched as the top of one suddenly burst upwards, spraying puss and purulent exudate high into the air, dropping with a splatter into the river below. It pulsed slowly as the deluge turned to a tickle, and then another burst, and another.

They saw innumerable twisted demonic things, billions upon billions of them, writhing and oozing; their monstrous bodies continually merging and separating, coalescing with the lake. It was impossible to see anything clearly, but as time seemed to have slowed down. Marco, at least, was able to determine that the closest *things* he could see resembled people. The smell was unbearable, it was worse than anything Marco could imagine. Miles was vomiting as he fell, his left eye now missing. Marco knew then all bets were off. Inside him he had a desire, a passion - a thirst for survival. He looked at Miles with new eyes. And he smiled a wicked smile.

Law of the jungle, it's kill or be killed.

Eventually they landed in the thickly viscous murky mustard-yellow river, not with a splash, but with a splat. It bubbled and boiled and pulsated. It seemed alive. It burned them and seeped into their very souls. And as they both tried desperately to stay on top of one another, they were aware of hideous figures bursting out and disappearing in a thick brownish froth. Mangled bodies beyond recognition slithered and bobbed as hands pulled at them from beneath the surface, from within the depths of their putrid home. Miles screamed and screamed, but Marco knew what he needed to do, he understood where he was and why he was here, and Lou watched him.

Lou sat on a bench now in soccer bleachers, eating popcorn. He felt the change in Marco and it pleased him. Surrounded by the many people Miles and Marco had wronged in their lifetime, including the many hookers they'd both had over the years. They were shouting and chanting like a group of cheerleaders and Lou sat back in delight as he watched Marco suddenly dominate the wretched Miles. A black cat pounced on something on the sand; he picked it up and leapt into Lou's lap, dropping it into his hand.

'What you find, boy?' He smiled. It was one of Mile's eyes. He turned to one of the hookers. 'Well, somebody's got to keep an eye on him.'

They all laughed with him.

Marco had got the upper-hand over Miles and was using him to stay afloat. Lou's head suddenly popped out behind them, he gargled in the vile liquid and then swallowed it with an, "Ahh."

He dropped back under and popped back out facing them. Marco had changed. He had accepted his situation and with that acceptance, he felt renewed. Deep within him, the minute evil that had driven him to this very ending, burst forth and he revelled in it. Lou nodded. Marco smiled back at him. He held Miles down under the liquid and felt him kick and buck as he did so. And then Marco howled in delight.

Lou grinned like a maniac bastard. Marco had discovered a new side, a new beginning and he would fit in well. The undiscovered country?

'Marco.' Lou yelled before he dropped back under, popping up behind them a few seconds later.

'Polo.'

The screen displays a classic 1960s horror typographic entitled:

"Revolting Tales: Episode Thirteen"

The episode starts with the camera looking through a window, into an office at two men in a violent quarrel.

We can't quite here what they are saying. The camera slowly pans towards a door and then slowly zooms in.

The door opens, and one of the men storms out, a bundle of papers under his arm. He doesn't bother closing the door behind him…

Episode Thirteen:

We're going to the movies

The Parish of St. Joseph

Father Ethan Swift was a boyish looking man of thirty-nine. He'd prepared well for the sermon he was about to deliver and he looked around as the various members of two families and friends all stood waiting. He lifted both hands. 'Please be seated.'

Father Ethan leant firmly on the pulpit, his fair skinned face firmly set. Respectful, compassionate, resolute in his determination to give comfort with the words he'd carefully written.

'The book of Job tells the story of a man who loved God and renounced evil.' He paused and allowed his eyes to move from mourner to mourner. Each of them in various stages of their own grief. They looked to him for the supporting words he believed he had written for them. His voice reverberated loud enough and he very rarely needed to use the built-in microphone and speakers.

In the centre of the isle, resting side by side, two coffins in a black and ivory livery were adorned with white lilies and yellow roses. In the front, brass stanchions with ornate ropes cordoned off the entrance. Either side stood a sign post with a picture of each of the deceased. A tribute of flowers and designed floral displays were carefully staged. There were two names written in white flowers. Marco and Miles.

The priest continued. 'Until one day, Lucifer posed a challenge to God. Test this man. Test his faith. When we mourn, we're all tempted to curse God. To give voice to our anger, our confusion, our sense of powerlessness against evil.' He paused to allow his words to sink in. He touched the Holy Book. 'We're tempted to ask, are we being punished for our own sins? We're tempted to ask, is there something we could have done differently? Why has God forsaken us?'

Some of the mourners quietly begin to cry.

'God has a plan for us. We may not understand it, because we are small and cannot understand his infinite wisdom, but like Job, who thought to question God. "Why?" he asks. "Why have you done this to me?" And God replied. "Who is this that darkens my counsel with words without knowledge? Who is ignorantly accusing me of doing wrong?" But God isn't angry with Job, nor with us for simply asking questions. God says, "Until you know a little more about running the physical universe, Job, don't tell me how to run the moral universe."' The priest stepped away from the pulpit and moved towards the two coffins. As he stood between them, he placed a hand on both.

'Job now knows that whatever has happened to him — in some way he can't fully understand — will work out for his benefit, for everyone's benefit. God's plan and purpose for our loved ones and for our lives are not subject to whims. We stand on the assurance written in the book of Isaiah, chapter forty-three verses one through three. "Fear not, for I have redeemed you; I have summoned you by name; you are mine. When you pass through the waters, I will be with you; and when you pass through the rivers, they will not sweep over you. When you walk through the fire, you will not be burned; the flames will not set you ablaze. For I am the Lord, your God." The untimely death of Marco and Miles is a source of misery for the loved ones they leave behind, but let us not despair, let us not fill our hearts with sorrow. For our brothers shall find their salvation in the arms our Lord, Jesus Christ. Amen.'

Thirty minutes later, after some quiet words with grieving parishioners, the church was empty. The priest closed the door and quietly walked towards the pulpit. As he ran an eye over the church he silently moved towards the prayer bench. Father Ethan bowed his head and carefully knelt. He closed his eyes and recited his prayers.

'I enjoyed your speech, Father.' A deep voice startled him and he looked up to find a smartly dressed figure, his back towards him, standing over the coffins. His first thoughts were the man had been in prayer and he'd missed him. Father Ethan stood and smiled. When the man turned and their faces met, their eyes locked, he saw the man - the shadow - for what it was, and Father Ethan's heart almost stopped. He knew the beast standing before him. He grabbed at his crucifix and took in a deep breath.

'You are not welcome in *His* house.'

The man smirked. 'I know.' He turned back to the coffins, and placed a hand on each of them.

Father Ethan did not move. He was deathly afraid.

'That story of Job, don't you find it just a little, insulting?'

'I trust in the Lord.'

A laugh. A laugh that started soft then gathered in volume and shook the room, it rumbled so loudly the building began to shake. Dust fell from the ceiling, the windows shattered, the large crucifix that adorned the body of Christ slipped from its fixture and fell, smashing to the ground. The two holy water fonts exploded, the water turned to steam. Father Ethan grabbed tightly to his cross but stood his ground. Eventually the laughter stopped, and with it the room settled. Father Ethan surveyed the devastation in terror. He looked down at the shattered Christ and drew strength from it.

'Why are you here, Lucifer?'

He turned and clasped his clawed hands behind his back. His visage was that of a man – a big man, dressed in a smart suit and a trench coat. There was distance between them, yet Father Ethan held onto his faith, he swallowed his fear.

'Why? Ethan, Ethan, what would your Lord say, hmm? Who is this who darkens my counsel with words without knowledge?'

'You're not here for my sermon.'

'No,' he chuckled. 'But I did like the passage you choose. Incidentally, your father, Gerry, says hi.'

'Lies. My father is *not* in hell.'

'No?'

'You sully his name by...' With supernatural speed the Beast was upon him, his large hands reaching for his face but never found it, they stopped inches away. A tongue of snakes burst out but hit an invisible barrier. The anger on Lucifer's face turned to a smile and he looked up. 'Friends in high places.' He ran a finger along the barrier. Father Ethan shook in fear, but held his head high.

'December twelfth, nineteen-eighty-three.'

Ethan blinked as Lucifer circled him. 'What?'

'You remember that date, don't you?'

'Yes, it's the day we moved to Connecticut.'

'You never thought to investigate why?'

'I will not listen to anymore. You are the father of lies.'

He nodded. 'True.'

He moved back to the coffins. 'These two, now there's a pair of boys even a mother would find hard pressed to love.' He ran a hand along Marco's casket. 'Now Marco, such a strong boy. I have a lot of plans for him. Miles… meh, well, he turned out to be wetter than you.' Lucifer pointed at the small puddle forming around Father Ethan's feet. 'Piss wet.'

Ethan, however, was not embarrassed by his fear. Emboldened, he stepped forward. 'Those two men will find the love of God waiting for them in his glorious…'

'Spare me,' Lucifer spat. 'Those two boys are mine now.' He strode towards him, his eyes burning. Father Ethan backed away despite his renewed faith.

'Does that comfort you?' He pointed to the cross in his hand. Father Ethan looked down and found he was holding a snake, its head reared up and hissed at him, but he resisted the urge to drop it, instead he held it closer to his chest.

Lucifer walked with a swagger, he rumbled a sermon of his own.

'What were you saying about Isaiah, Ethan? Fear not, for I have liberated you; I have summoned you by name, Ethan; you are mine.' He continued to saunter towards him, he was in no hurry, Ethan however, his heart racing, backed up along the aisle that led to the main doors. He looked down to see the snake had twisted itself around his arm and the head bit deeply into his skin, he cried out in pain and hurried towards the door.

'When you pass through the purifying pustules of my Kingdom, Ethan, I will be with you. When you pass through the rivers, they will devour you, they will fuck you dry, and when you walk through my fire, you will be burned beyond death; the flames will set your soul ablaze. For I am your Lord.'

'I will not be in your kingdom, Lucifer, Angel of Evil. I am loved by God, protected by Him. I bath in his glory and pity you for you can never know his love.'

Lucifer poured fire onto him, but when the flames subsided, Ethan remained untouched. 'You know nothing little man. I may not be able to touch you, Ethan, but I will be back for you. December twelfth.' And with a gesture, he pulled the church down on top of him. Father Ethan lay prostrate as Lucifer leered over him. 'You can have the carcasses, send them to Him gift wrapped if you like; I've already got their souls. I'll be seeing you again soon, Ethan.'

Father Ethan coughed and blood burst from his lips. The snake burrowed into his arm and he screamed again at it. He hadn't the strength to fight it off and in horror watched it slip up underneath his skin.

'Until December twelfth, Ethan.'

He looked up at the sky. Sirens could be heard in the distance.

Father Ethan openly sobbed.

Newton Brown Television Studio

'I'm telling you, we're screwed, Jack. That writer just threw his toys and walked; now we don't *have* a fucking script. No script. No show! It's that simple.' Will Sampago was shaking as he bellowed down the receiver. He walked around his desk seven times during the entire conversation. As a hefty man of fifty-eight, he was, according to just about everyone, a prime candidate for a heart attack, and yet, despite people telling him this for the last fifteen years, he was just as highly strung.

'Don't tell me to calm down, Jesus Christ. What the fuck do you want me to do, Jack? I'm ready. The studio is ready. I'm paying people to stand around; I need a god-damn script!' Will pulled out his electronic cigarette and furiously puffed at it. It didn't calm him. He threw it at the wall. He covered the receiver and shouted, 'Jackie! Get me a real fucking cigarette, now.' Jack was still talking when he put the phone back to his ear.

'No! There's no way we can negotiate with him. He won't let us change anything. Fucking writers, they don't understand we can't always make things look like the way they describe it in a book. Hold on Jack.' He turned to the door. 'Jackie!'

She burst into his office and handed him a pack of Marlboro lights.

'Lights? Jesus Christ, Jackie.'

'It's all I had, Will. I'm sorry.'

'Get out!' He pulled the filter off one and lit it. The feel of actual smoke flowing through his lungs, warming his throat, made him feel marginally better. 'Yeah I'm still here, Jack.' He sighed. Then something Jack said made him roar again. 'Oh just make something up? Oh real fucking genius, Jack, and who's gonna write it, you? Jesus

Christ. You just get down here with a fucking script, or I'll tell everyone what a miserable shit you were over, Tracey, and how she screwed every man on set, because even with the pills and a pump your dick was too fucking small for her to feel a god-damn thing.' He slammed the phone down hard and cracked the case.

'Fuck!'

There was a knock at the door.

'What!'

It opened and in walked an efficient looking woman.

'And who the fuck are you?'

He couldn't help but notice she was carrying a bundle of paper. She walked right up to him and placed it in his hand. 'You wanted a script I believe?'

'Listen lady…'

'Sandra.'

'Okay, Sandra. Listen, sweetheart, I don't have any time right now to negotiate a deal, I'm behind on a project and it's costing me millions, so if you'd be so kind...'

'There's no negotiation. It's yours. Do what you want with it. Use it, re-write it, burn it. Your choice.' She walked away. He calmed down as he read the title: *Revolting Tales*. 'Who owns the copyright, Sandra?'

She turned with a smile. 'Apparently you do, Will.' And she walked away, quietly closing the door.

He picked up his phone but it was no longer working.

'Jackie, get me Jack on the phone right now!'

* * *

'Will, we've set up the first scene. I've got lighting down and they're all ready, but production says we need to get a lifter in to hoist up some of the bodies, cos the way we've been doing it ain't safe.'

Will nodded. 'Fine, let's just get it done, like now. Time is money, people.' He shouted out, 'I want the first and second crew in here shooting two scenes at once. We need to make up for lost time.' He walked towards a group of crew huddled around a small screen. 'How's it looking?'

A tall blonde kid turned. 'Looking great, boss. We've piled as many cars as we could get into the shot.'

'I want more. Use as much as you can, fill it. I want cars, doors, glass, fucking anything. It's gotta look full, you get me?'

'I get you, boss.' He grabbed the handheld speaker and started bellowing orders to the crew. Will spotted the "fx" guys at their truck. He jogged over to them. 'Frank, how we doing on the blood pools?'

Smiling he pulled out a large box and opened it.

'Fourteen silicone blood pools. They look real, don't they?'

'Oh beautiful, Frank. Real nice. Good job.' He walked back towards the monitors and was intercepted by a man dressed in a dirty overcoat, a cigarette dangling from his puffy face. He held up the script.

'What's my motivation, Will?'

They walked together as Will detailed it for him. 'Okay Johnny...'

'Call me Bob, I'm in character.'

'Right. Bob. You're walking up to the scene of the call out, you and your partner. You don't know anything yet, so you're going in blind. When you get closer, you'll see Lucy...'

'The reporter, right, she's playing Sara?'

'Yeah, she's gonna start asking you for information and this that and everything else, you know the way they always do.'

'Me and Sara, we have history, right?'

Will sighed. 'Jesus, Jonny, have you read the fucking script?'

'Yeah, yeah, of course I've read it. I just wanna understand it.'

'Okay listen, they've known each other since grade school, okay? Even dated for a bit in high school. She only tolerates him because Bob is still very good friends with her husband. It's a very small town, you get that?'

'Would he really say, "why do I have to smell your unwashed lady parts"?'

'Jesus Chris, Jonny, I don't have time...' He rubbed his forehead. 'Well why don't you go and run through it with Lucy, okay? Go.'

Jonny nodded and called Lucy over. Will laughed despite the anxiety he was feeling.

Thirty minutes later, the set was finished. Cameras were primed at ready. Lighting was set. Will sat in a chair facing the block of monitors. He puffed on his cigarette.

'Okay everyone into position?'

There was quiet on the set. 'Action!'

A car pulled up and the camera focused on the man stepping out of the driver's side door. As he surveys the area, he spots the reporter and camera crew moving towards him. He puts up his hand in a "stop right there" motion. The reporter steps forward.

'I have nothing for you right now, Sara.'

She pouts. 'Oh, come on, Bob, you have to give me something. Why do I have to go through this begging routine with you every time something good happens?'

'Why do I have to smell your un.. un-washed... Your...' Laughing erupted on set. Jonny dropped his head and then looked up. 'I'm sorry, Will. Can we go again?'

'Cut!' Will had turned a shade of red. 'Pull it to-fucking-gether, Jonny. Jesus. Reset people. Back to the car!'

Several hours later, after a few false starts, the first set of filming had completed.

'That's a wrap people, good job!' Will rubbed his hands and turned to the production manager. 'How we doing with the bar scene, Jim?'

'It's almost there, just gotta finish the décor, get the wall of bottles done, you know, fill them with the right coloured liquids, that sort of thing. They're eating lunch right now.'

'Lunch?' Will sighed. 'Jim, I want that scene ready in one hour, no excuses. I don't care if you have to get every man woman and child, including me, to piss in a fucking bottle, just get it done. We don't got time for lunches.'

Jim nodded and hurried away.

'Am I the only person here who understands the concept of time?'

Fairfield, Connecticut

Father Ethan knelt at the grave of his father and put a shaky hand on the tombstone. It had been some months since his encounter with Lucifer but he continually ran over the conversation in his mind, and like every day previous, he recalled it as if it just happened. It consumed him.

The church was still under construction. But he found he just couldn't face the prospect of preaching there, so he left, moved to another parish, hoping he could rebuild his life, possibly to reconsider his choices. Over time his faith wavered, but his protection against the powers of Satan, clearly from God, reminded him of just how powerful his "friends in high places" were. Was he being tested, in the same way as Job? It was possible and because he understood the story, far better than Job ever did, he knew he *had* to keep his head held high, not give in to the clear temptations being laid out before him.

That, however, didn't stop the nightmares, and it never could.

Why did Lucifer suggest his father would be in hell? Was it just another lie? A temptation? Just what was the purpose of it? Was it simply to sow the seed of doubt?

Well if that was true, he thought, *it had done its job.*

Despite every instinct that told him to just let God give him the direction he needed, he couldn't help but think dark thoughts. In all his time as a priest, in all the years he'd served God faithfully, he'd never once been granted the privilege of seeing a Divine-Being. It was odd then that his first and only encounter was with Satan. There was something terribly wrong there. He released the grip on the tombstone and walked back down the path towards his new church, his new home.

It wasn't a very comforting place.

Ethan was aware of how dark it became. He'd lost track of the time. Slowly he ambled back, ascended the stairs to the old church and was gratified to see Father McGuigan smile at his approach. He was a man in his late seventies, white haired, lined with age. Irish with a passion.

'Good evening to you, Father Ethan.'

Ethan smiled. 'Good evening, Father.'

It was a cold night and they entered the church together, the older man bolted the door. 'Come to the fire, Ethan.'

They sat and warmed by it in quiet contemplation. McGuigan frowned, he could tell the young man was having crises of some kind, whether it was an issue of faith, or unrelated to the church, he couldn't tell but his fatherly nature, his need to be the shepherd compelled him to speak.

'You seem troubled, son. Tell me, what's on your mind?'

'Satan,' Ethan replied looking outward through the window towards the graveyard at McGuigan silence, he turned to him and smiled sadly. He watched as the old man gave a quick sign of the cross and kissed his crucifix. At length he spoke. 'That's enough to make any man's heart heavy, even an old man who's seen the worst of wicked in this world. Why are you thinking of him, Ethan?'

'Because…' he looked directly into McGuigan's old grey eyes. 'Because he came to me in my church.'

Father McGuigan gave a sharp intake of breath. It said it all and Ethan sighed.

'That's how the building fell?' McGuigan asked.

'He pulled it down on top of me, yes.'

He reached over and patted the younger man's hand. 'God was with you, my son, he protected you.'

'From Him, yes. Not from myself.'

'You survived, Ethan, with nothing more than what? A few scrapes and bruises?'

'And this,' he pulled up his right sleeve. A black snakelike mark was burnt into his skin, inflamed and raw. McGuigan grabbed at it, it burned his hand. He let go in an instant more in shock than pain.

'By all that is unholy!' he cried. 'He marked you.'

Ethan nodded and covered his arm. 'I have prayed each day for healing, but it gets worse as times goes by.'

'Come with me!' McGuigan said and grabbed him by his coat. He followed hurriedly through the old church and ran at times, to keep up with the surprisingly spry older priest. They reached an ornately decorated room, deep inside the church. When they were inside, Father McGuigan bolted the doors; he held a hand to his heaving chest. When he had the breath to do so, he spoke.

'We must evict this evil from you.'

Ethan nodded. He hoped the old man had something other than prayer. That had done nothing so far.

'Follow me, Ethan.'

They walked through the room into the back and then entered an old musty antechamber. Through this they came to an inner sanctum of sorts. A place Ethan had never visited. It was small, frugally decorated, but the tell-tale signs that someone, clearly McGuigan, occupied and made frequent use of it. Ethan sat down with a weary heart into a wooden chair beside an empty table. He laid his arm out onto it. McGuigan paced up and down for a moment in deep thought. Eventually he moved over to the door and locked it. Putting the key into the pocket of his robe he said, 'We should pray, uninterrupted, first.'

Together they recited prayer after prayer. Eventually Ethan asked him:

'How do we remove the mark?'

Father McGuigan was leaning into an old chest by the wall. 'Oh, I have something here that will help, if I can only find it,' he said as he rummaged inside. With an exclamation he pulled out a large red-velvet bag. 'Here it is. I found it. This, Ethan, this is the answer.'

Father Ethan looked inquisitively at it. 'What's in the bag, Father?'

McGuigan pulled open the string and carefully pulled out a very shiny looking meat-clever. Ethan looked at him in concern. 'Father?'

Before Ethan's eyes, he watched as McGuigan transformed from a warm and friendly man, to a nightmare in holy robe. His eyes turned completely black. His skin was whiter than snow, almost translucent. 'Stay still, son.' His voice had changed to a cackled-raspy whisper. 'I will purify you with my blade.'

He lunged at Ethan who instinctively rolled away. The head of the cleaver buried itself deep into the table. McGuigan's eyes had become almost metallic; his movement became more and more frantic. He dislodged the cleaver with little effort, but in the time it took to do so, Ethan got to his feet and moved quickly towards the door. Desperately he tried in-vain to open it. It was locked, he remembered, McGuigan had locked it and pocketed the key. The old man rushed forward.

Ethan barely had any time to defend himself. 'Father, please!'

'It's okay, Ethan, shhh, this will all be over soon.' He lunged again. Ethan cried out as he fell backwards onto the floor. The old priest was quickly upon him, gnashing yellow teeth, drooling saliva, laughing hysterically, maniacally at him. He continued to brandish the cleaver, unsuccessful he tried again to bury it into Ethan's arm.

Father Ethan again tried a direct appeal. 'Stop, Father, please!' There was no stopping the zombie like creature that had taken over his old friend's form. He pushed hard with his feet and the old priest flew back against the wall with a crash. He fell to the floor hard, but with the fluidity of a Kung-Fu master, he flipped back onto his feet and with a speed that shocked the younger man, he rushed back at him, again laughing hysterically. His unintelligibly shouting and yelling was chilling. He swung the blade in random directions. He had no other purpose but to kill or maim. He screamed curses, gurgled, cackled, and the blade got just a little closer every time. Eventually it connected, nicking his forehead. In panic, Ethan grabbed at a wooden chair. He swung it in front of him, into the path of the raging maniac, but the cadaverous old priest effortlessly batted it aside and it smashed to smithereens against the wall. Ethan scuttled away, but not fast enough. The blade hit. It buried itself deep into his left shoulder. Ethan howled in pain as the old priest disengaged it, and brought it down again. All the time shrieking.

Ethan felt the pain rip through him. He tried to buy time. 'For God sake, Father! This isn't you. Fight it.'

'Oh, you think your *Father* will save you again?' In a shrill voice he looked up to the heavens and shouted: 'Arise, O Lord; save me, O my God: for thou hast smitten all mine enemies upon the cheek bone; thou hast broken the teeth of the ungodly.' Laughing again, he swung the blade over and over.

But Ethan had used the time wisely and grabbed a large chunk of broken wood from the remains of the chair and he used it to fend off the ferocious attack of his elder. He saw the old priest was no longer himself, knew some evil had taken him and he wondered how it had been done. Lucifer had been unable to touch him, yet he somehow corrupted McGuigan.

The cadaverous priest hurled foul abuse at him.

'I'll drown you in your own piss and then I'll shit in your cock-sucking mouth, you prurient little prick. Down, down you'll go, into the river of puss, and before Him you'll swallow all the cocks in Hell. The seed of the demons will fill you until you burst, as you deserve; he will fuck you until you're nothing more than dust. You'll burn with him, you'll burn with me!' He swung the cleaver again and it narrowly missed his head. He cried out as the blade caught his elbow. Ethan shook in pain and fear. The old priest suddenly stiffened. His eyes cleared and he looked down at the wreck of the man he'd been trying to kill, he dropped the blade to the floor in confusion.

'Ethan…?'

But Ethan failed to notice his transformation. Too preoccupied with saving his own life, he took the confusion as a sign to act. With a feral scream he rammed the broken chair leg right through the old man's chest. With a cough of blood he looked down at the wooden stake protruding from him. His shaking hand tried to touch it, but it was too much for the old man, who staggered back mouth agape, eyes wide. He looked down at Ethan, blood seeped from his mouth.

'Why...?' he gurgled, and then his eyes rolled up into his head and he fell backwards, landing on the floor with a thud. He twitched and convulsed, coughed and spluttered, the breaths now agonal and various sized bubbles of blood developed and popped around his nose and mouth. A puddle of urine pooled around him, his muscles twitched infrequently in spasm.

Ethan continued to stare long after the priest was dead. A rumble of thunder reverberated loudly throughout the church and Ethan finally crawled over to him murmuring. 'Dear God, what have I done...?'

There was silence.

The clock chimed in the hallway twelve times.

It was midnight.

Midnight. The twelfth of December.

He looked down at the prone form, the chair leg still buried deep into his chest and in that moment Ethan knew what had happened.

He'd killed a man. Not a monster. At the moment Ethan thrust the chair leg through the old unaware priest. Whatever evil possessed him had gone. And yet, he still didn't understand what just happened. He sobbed uncontrollably.

To take a life was a sin. There was no getting past it; he'd murdered Father McGuigan – but unintentionally.

'Father,' he cried to the heavens, 'forgive me!' Again there was a violent clap of thunder. Ethan shakily searched the dead priest's pockets for the key, and as he found it, he heard the door creak open. He looked up sharply as a man slipped in. He wore a bright orange jogging suit and purple sneakers; in his right hand he held a thirty-two ounce "big-gulp" cup of soda.

'I hope this isn't a bad moment?' Without waiting for an answer, he walked in and quietly closed the door. Ethan clutched his crucifix firmly. He backed away and screamed as something cold and clammy clamped firmly around his ankle. It was Father McGuigan's dead hand.

Lucifer sucked on the straw of his soda. 'You've been a naughty, naughty, boy, Ethan.'

'You have no power over me, Lucifer.' He held his cross in defiance, but even to his ears, his words sounded hollow.

Lucifer smiled and put down his cup. 'Call me Lou.'

Ethan kicked hard but could not release the dead priest's hold. McGuigan jerked his hand violently, and Ethan lost his balance and he fell backwards onto the floor. He lay there, winded. Swiftly Lou was above him, his giant face inches from his own. Ethan cried out in horror and grabbed at his cross, thrusting it into Lou's face. A clawed hand ripped it from him and he ate it, spitting splinters of wood back at him. Lou's face begun to change; it grew larger, bull like, his skin bright red. A large golden ring formed through his wide nose and his eyes turned a burning yellow the pupil of which elongated vertically. He snorted puffs of smoke from his nostrils and he reached down and took Ethan by the neck and face. He slowly twisted his head this way and that.

'Looks like someone lost his friends.'

And in a flash he was gone. Ethan stared upwards murmuring, 'Why have you forsaken me, O lord?' He suddenly jerked, shifting position; he looked up to see Lou, his back to him, dragging him by the ankle towards a wall. He was whistling tunelessly as he gestured towards it. It opened showing only darkness beyond. He pulled Ethan through the wall and it closed behind them. Ethan could only watch as he found himself in a dark secluded alleyway. The only light came from a flashing neon sign: *Caesar's Palace*.

'We're going to have soooo much fun, Father, you, me, oh, and Gerry – we mustn't forget Gerry.' He continued to drag him towards a dumpster and as they passed behind it, Father Ethan Swift cried as a putrescent stench violently assaulted him.

Lou turned, still holding his ankle. 'You do understand why you're here, don't you, Ethan?'

Ethan's eyes were puffy-red. He could not find any words, he was too terrified.

Lou slipped down beside him and whispered, 'But the fearful, and unbelieving, and the abominable, and murderers, and fornicators, and sorcerers, and idolaters, and all liars, shall have their part in the lake, which burns with fire and brimstone: which is the second death…'

'I was defending myself.'

'Not when you committed the act, Ethan. He was defenceless, a confused old man. You ran him through, Ethan, with anger and hatred. An innocent – of sorts – it was a beautiful thing to watch.'

'But he would have killed me.'

'That was your test, Ethan. Where would you be now, if he had done so?'

'I failed the basic test of faith...'

'Shhh,' a clawed finger touched his lips lightly. 'I might have been a little naughty, Father McGuigan lost his faith years ago – he didn't have the friends you... had.'

Ethan choked a sob. 'What happens to me now?'

Lou seemed to think for a moment. 'I'm not sure what I'm going to do with you yet, Ethan.' He picked him up by the neck. There was a large clap of thunder, and Lou scowled at the sky. He turned back to him. 'I'm not short of ideas though. Why don't you catch up with Marco and Miles while I think things over, maybe they'd like to hear your sermon?' Before he could respond, Lou threw him high into the air and he screamed, and screamed, as he flailed. Below him, he could see the purulent river, a ginormous dragon-fly bathed him in fire and his holy clothes instantly disintegrated.

Naked and soulless, he fell from *on high*.

Newton Brown Television Studio

'It will look much better once we have the backdrop lighting and so on,' production assistant, Mary Talbot remarked, her head down low, alongside Will's. The intricate details of the model ship were really quite impressive, Will mused. His eyes turned to Mary and he stood and sniffed.

'It's okay, I suppose.' Mary smiled without looking at him. She knew he'd like it.

He eyed her suspiciously. 'This isn't the usual garbage the studio chucks out, not on the budget we have, so where'd you get it, Mary?'

'We found a place, not far from here. Some guy called Lou owns one of those "all in one" places, you know the type: "bait and tackle, shoe repairs, model making, groceries, sex shop". Jake was browsing some models he had and when he mentioned we were looking for a ship, the guy gave him this. Jake said it was better than anything they could do on such short notice, so I said buy it.' She looked hesitantly at him. He bent down again and looked onto the deck then abruptly turned his head. He looked sharp.

'How much?'

'Nothing.'

'Come again?'

'Seriously. He didn't want anything for it. Said some guy had ordered and paid for it, but never collected. Apparently it'd been sitting in his shop for several months,' she said coughing. 'So I took the chance that for free, you know, you might like it.'

'For free, I fucking love it.' Will smiled at her. 'Good work, Mary. Get it over to the *fx* guys.'

She grabbed the model and left.

* * *

It had been a very difficult first few days on the set, primarily because no one really had time to read the script, or fully absorb it. The "fx" guys had been far luckier and quickly drafted a number of local kids to help build sets out of anything they could find lying around the old studio. Will had really got things back on track. His bullish approach never failed to motivate the people who worked for him, all being paid meagre wages. All waiting for the "big one", that one film to make them all rich. Will knew they were deluding themselves. Nothing that ever came out of this particular studio made any more than the costs to produce it, and they were all B horror television episodes anyway, aired on quiet networks, usually at two or three in the morning. The actors weren't even particularly good, and the stories were equally as bad. How they'd even managed to stay on air surprised him, but it wasn't his job to worry about it and had this been just another one of these poorly written scripts by some upstart of an author, who was just trying to get his name on screen. He'd have felt the same as he always did. But this wasn't turning out like that.

Will had been very impressed with what the script team had done with the stories that fell into his lap. So impressed in fact, he quietly admitted to himself he was actually excited. How that woman knew they were desperate or what had happened to her after she left his office, really didn't bother Will as much as it should have. He'd been given break after break; no authors, no costs, free models, a good team. There may be profit in the series yet.

Will picked up the phone and dialled.

'Frank? Will. Listen, I want to go over the next few scenes with you. I've just had a good idea with the boat story, and I want to add a sequence with a helicopter. Yeah, I saw the model. What did you think? Yeah my thoughts exactly. I was thinking we might set up a camera to pan around it then transfer it into the computer, green screen the cockpit so we can put different sequences in later, possible? Okay great. Speak soon.' He replaced the receiver and paused. After a moment's thought he picked it up and dialled again.

'Jim? Will. Did you finish that bar set yet..? Beautiful, I'm on my way.'

The River of Puss, Hell

Ethan lay naked on what he decided was a rock. The heat around him was intense but that didn't bother him. Oddly it wasn't even uncomfortable. Resting on his elbows, looking out at his purulent home, he watched as billions of creatures writhed and screamed. An unintelligible babble of voices filled the air, yet despite his inability to understand them, the universal sound of people in hopeless agony was unmistakable. He watched as another screaming *thing* floated by, and another. He couldn't really tell how long he'd been there, or how many monstrous things he'd counted. Mutated creatures, an amalgam of animals and men, dragonfly people, deer, it was just too horrific – and yet – Ethan was no longer afraid. He heard a gurgle below him and it jolted him from his reverie. He leaned over and saw a man, one of his eyes missing, desperately trying to cling to the rock. Ethan immediately reached down and grabbed at his arm. He instinctively screamed and flailed, threatening to pull Ethan in with him, but something about the panic and fear, the total dread on the poor fellows face, spurred Ethan into action.

'Don't struggled, I'll help you.'

The man had not heard him. He was too locked into his own terror to understand any words.

Ethan jerked violently to get his attention. He shouted at him, 'Stop struggling!'

The man's eye focused and he finally complied. A small part of his fragmented mind understood the instruction he was given. He allowed himself to be helped out of the river. Burning slime oozed from his naked form, and Ethan pulled with all his might at the dead weight. Eventually, panting, he pulled the man completely free, and stood above him, as he lay on the rock. Neither of them spoke for the longest time. Ethan sat up and examined the newcomer. His body covered in boils and pustules and scars.

'Can you speak?' Ethan asked.

The man turned his head and simply stared at him – through him. The pupil of his eye a mere pin-prick. Ethan shaded his face and watched as it slowly dilated.

'Well, you're one eye works okay, that's a good sign. My name is Ethan.' He looked out at the horizon, volcanoes of boils as far as the eye could see.

'I wish I knew how long I've been here,' he said and sighed to himself. Then he looked down at the man lying prone. He knelt down beside him.

'I cannot imagine what you've seen, but I hope there's some vestige of humanity left in you, some part of you that remembers who you once were.' The man curled himself into a foetal position. Ethan reached over and stroked his hair. 'You poor man.' He looked up to the sky, but there was no comfort to be found in that burning haze of rolling flames.

'We're stuck here for all eternity, you and me, and billions of other poor souls.' He lowered his head and slowly shook it. 'And my only companion can't even speak.'

He made a gurgled sound. 'Mm...' Ethan looked at him quickly.

'Mma..' His tongue flopped awkwardly in his mouth, as he was struggling to remember how to form words.

'Mmaaaa...' He forced a hand into his mouth and started to pull at his tongue. Ethan instantly held him as he started to cough uncontrollably. He forced him upright, patting hard on his back. He suddenly vomited violently, a stream of puss and god knows what else splattered against the rock. Ethan, still holding him, looked sharply away. The man was convulsing now, his hands desperately pulling at his tongue - pulling it out. Ethan had a hard time turning the man's head, because he was kicking and bucking so hard, but when he finally managed it, he saw it wasn't his tongue, but something else - something slimy and thick, spongy and pulsating, and something very large. He quickly grabbed at it too. The two of them now, pulled and pulled and with the addition of Ethan's strength, a slug like creature slowly began to protrude from inside the man's swollen throat. It fought against them but with hardly any purchase, it was only a matter of time before they got it out. The man began to kick and jerk even more violently in terror, more than pain, and Ethan gritted his teeth, straining, determined to rid the man of the disgusting mollusc like invader. It was slimy and spongy-soft, difficult to hold, but somehow Ethan managed to get a better hold of it, and as it protruded further, he was able to finally wrap a strong hand on it. With all the strength he could muster, he pulled until the vile creature flew out, hitting the rock with a wet thump. They both scuttled away as fast as they could. The creature flipped in the heat of the flaming sky, opened what could only be described as a mouth, and shrieked so loudly, both men had to cover their ears. Finally it launched off the rock and disappeared into the current of the river.

'Miles...' the man said, coughing, holding his throat. Weakly he said, 'My name is, Miles.' And with that he began to cry hysterically. Ethan knew this man. He had given a sermon at his passing almost a year previous. He pulled Miles into a tight hug and rocked him until his cries began to subside.

Miles wiped at his face and nose with the back of his hand. 'Thank you.' His voice was raspy. The creature obviously did damage to his throat.

'You don't need to thank me, Miles.' Ethan's sad face looked around.

'What's your name?' Miles croaked.

'Ethan. Ethan Swift.'

'How long have you been here?'

He shrugged. 'I have no idea, Miles. Not quite as long as you.'

'Time has no meaning in this place.' He sniffed again. 'A minute could be a year. It feels like I've been here forever.'

'At least a year, by my understanding.'

Miles frowned. 'How could you know that?'

'Well, believe it or not, I buried you.'

'Oh.'

Ethan studied Miles for a moment, eventually he voiced a concern. 'You're not breathing.'

'I'm dead, aren't I? Dead people don't breath.'

'True, but Miles, if you're dead, and we're both here in Hell, then I'm dead too, right?'

Miles snorted. 'I guess.'

'Then how come I'm still breathing?'

'I don't know.' They stood together. 'One thing's for sure, Ethan, this rock was never here before, I'd have remembered, trust me. You were lucky to find it.'

'Lucky? I wonder.' Ethan thought hard. *Why am I still breathing? What purpose does it serve me? I'm dead, in Hell, taken by Lucifer – or Lou. Why am I still breathing? How did I get onto the rock? Was I really just lucky enough to find the only visible rock in this disgusting, vile space? The only safe haven? Why would Lou allow that? I should just be one of billions of poor creatures, like Miles, perpetually drowning – but I'm not. Was this part of his game?*

Miles had been talking but Ethan hadn't heard a word.

'…then that's when we got here, Marco and me.'

'I'm sorry, Miles, what?'

Miles sighed quietly and dropped his gaze. 'Nothing.'

'Listen, Miles. I have a strong suspicion that we aren't meant to be here.'

Miles looked at him oddly, and then he involuntarily giggled, that giggle turned into a full belly laugh. Eventually he stopped. 'Thank you, Ethan, that's the first time I've laughed in… well I don't remember.'

But Ethan wasn't paying attention. Ethan wanted the answer to a question searing the synapses of his brain. *Why am I still breathing?*

Newton Brown Television Studio

Will sat in the front row of the cinema viewing room, completely captured by the story unfolding on the screen before him. Alongside him sat Mary. As the credits finally rolled, he sat back into the soft chair and slowly nodded. A smile spread across his usually cheerless face.

'Seriously Mary, that's amazing. We've got a beauty right there. I can't believe what you did with that.'

Mary pulled out a packet of cigarettes and offered him one. He briefly hesitated before he eventually took it. She lit his and then hers and they both blew smoke up into the room.

He enjoyed smoking. 'Has Jack seen this yet?'

Mary shook her head. 'We didn't want anyone to see it before you.'

Will smiled. A genuine smile and Mary smirked. She knew that look.

'You wanna do me here, or in the sound booth?'

'Maybe later,' he held her hand. 'This is the best shit we've ever done.'

She nodded. 'Well, it's usually just shit, so…'

He leaned in and kissed her, hard. The suddenness of it surprised her. Their teeth hit together as he pushed his tongue to hers. She grabbed his head with her left hand, and held her smoke away with the other. When he pulled away, she pouted. 'Fuck, Will, don't stop there.'

'Later. I'll find you.' He stood and adjusted his pants.

At the back of the cinema, hidden in darkness, Lou and Sandra sat eating popcorn. They watched as Will and Mary left the room.

Sandra had an evil expression on her sour face. 'This is going to rock their world, Lou.'

He nodded, and then, in a perfect mimic of the scene they'd both just witnessed, Lou grabbed Sandra by her head and pushed his long tongue into her wide mouth. Sandra, however, simply pulled out a large knife from her pocketbook and pushed it deep into Lou's crotch. He pulled out his tongue, she twisted it sharply as they locked eyes, and he sighed.

'You know how to give a demon a good time, Sandra.'

They continued to look deeply into each other's eyes as she pulled it out. She wiped his blood on her skirt, and neatly placed it back into her pocketbook.

'I know,' she said.

Dodge Plymouth Car Dealership, Madison – Connecticut

Bob Snook held up one hand in a *stop right there motion* to the reporter as he walked by.

'I have nothing for you right now, Sara.'

'Oh, come on, Bob, you have to give me something. Why do I have to go through this begging routine with you every time something good happens?'

With barely a passing second Bob replied: 'Why do I have to smell your unwashed lady parts?'

'Oh! Was that really necessary?' A disgusted looked passed over her face.

'Hope the camera wasn't on just then.' Bob continued to walk to the scene and Sara followed.

'It was, so Ha! Maybe I'll air that comment, Bob.'

Bob paused and she almost bumped into him. 'Yeah, well ya might want to think about that, kiddo. Do you really want to air a comment about your smelly snatch? That reputation could ruin your chance at the big time.' He continued walking.

'You really are a flaming asshole, ya know that, Bob.'

'Why, fuck you very much, Sara.'

'Bob!' Sara screamed. He stopped and sighed.

'Okay, turn that fuckin' thing on.' Bob sucked in his gut and tucked in his shirt. Sara motioned to the cameraman to hurry and she got ready with the microphone. The cameraman motioned a *go* sign and Sara spoke.

'Detective Snook, what can you tell us about this beyond bizarre situation?'

Bob spoke with his best Walter Brimley impersonation: 'Anything that I may say at this point, so early into this case, without further investigation, would be purely speculation. And I'm not going to do that so…. fuck you very much.'

Sara lowered her microphone in defeat. 'You really are a cock-sucker, you know that, Bob.'

Bob smiled, then reached over and gave Sara a peck on the cheek. 'Why do you bother wearing a bra anyway?'

The cameraman chuckled. Sara looked down briefly at her extremely small breasts, again in defeat. Bob reached the crime scene tape and ducked underneath it. He was met by one of his detectives.

'Morning, Robert.' Detective Foito handed him a Starbucks coffee.

'This is one for the record books, buddy. I am completely clueless here.'

'You're always clueless, Don, there's nothing new there.' Bob sipped from the coffee and smiled. 'Thanks.' He looked up for the first time at the scene without expression. There in the showroom of the Madison Dodge Plymouth Car Dealership was mayhem of disaster. New cars were twisted and tangled in amongst each other. Cars on top of cars, four high, smashed glass, and metal of all kinds piled everywhere. Cars through walls, piled up to the ceiling, some upside down, some cut completely in half. It looked like a scrap medal junkyard, but with new cars. In addition to all the mayhem of metal, there was evidence of blood. A lot of it. And guts, and shit, and body parts. None of which were connected to any of the bodies. There were lots of those too.

Bob took another sip of his coffee and watched as a photo tech suddenly slipped and fell to the floor. As he thrashed desperately, trying to get up, his panic increased tenfold as he'd now covered himself in one of the pools of blood. Bob walked over to him just as he got to his feet.

'It's blood so get used to it. Accept it and now do your fuckin' job without further screwing up my crime scene.'

The tech mumbled an apology and hurried away.

'Pretty wild, eh, Robert?' Don approached and stood to Bob's right.

He sighed heavily. 'I *was* hoping it wouldn't reach us, at least until after I retired.'

'So you think this is linked to all the others?' Don seemed surprised.

Bob frowned at him. 'Come on Don, really?' He pointed to the mayhem.

'Wow.' Don ignored the sarcasm. 'So what now Sarge, we call the Feds, CIA, what?'

Bob took another sip of his coffee and looked at his watch. 'No need for that.'

Almost on cue, as if it had been planned in some way, a helicopter flew by, catching everyone's attention, everyone but Bob, who was more interested in the scene. It landed in the adjoining Ford Dealership parking lot. FBI clearly displayed on the doors.

'Did you get separate samples for me like I asked you on the phone earlier?'

'Of course I did, Sarge, you know me better than that. No troubles.'

'Yeah, well I also know how you think with your dick too, and you know how that always gets you in trouble. Still fuckin' that fat chick?'

Don beamed. 'Ah, yup. Nothing like em, Sarge.'

Bob winced and simply shook his head.

'Don't knock it till ya try it, Sarge.' Don laughed. 'Fat chicks deserve lovin' too, ya know?'

Wishing the conversation over, Bob said, 'Let me know as soon as you get an ID on the bodies.'

'Sure thing, my friend.' Don walked away.

Bob continued assessing the scene. Although he didn't show it, he was completely perplexed and at a total loss. Nothing made sense. It defied all reason and logic. It was simply impossible, but yet, there it was. Then his confusion turned to relief as he heard a voice approaching from behind.

'Good morning, Detective Snook.'

He didn't turn. He just sipped his coffee. Special Agent Mark O'Conner stood beside him.

'No need to say anything, Mark, it's all yours.'

O'Conner did not remove his regulation sunglasses. 'Cops usually hate it when the Feds come in and take a case from the locals, Detective. You actually seemed relieved.'

'Oh I'm *more* than willing to hand this one over, Mark.'

Special Agent O'Conner removed his glasses. He leaned in and Bob raised an eyebrow. 'Not this time, Detective. The situation is now global. We don't have the man power or the resources to do it ourselves. We need all the help we can get.'

Bob laughed. 'Yeah right, I'm not gonna be your coffee boy, O'Conner.'

'I don't drink coffee.' He slipped his glasses back on and put his hands on his hips. He looked around the scene briefly. 'It's your case Snook, whether you like it or not.' Both were silent as they continued to survey the mayhem around them.

Bob spoke first. 'What can you tell me, Mark?' His tone had turned more cordial.

Mark responded in kind. 'There is *nothing* classified anymore, Bob. We are all circling a toilet bowl and it's about to get flushed.'

'Great.'

They shook hands. Mark headed back to his ride. As he left he called out over his shoulder. 'Keep me up to date, Bob.'

'Of course,' he replied, but Mark had already gone.

Bob took a deep breath and entered the showroom. He was careful where he walked thinking about the shitter the tech took minutes prior. He walked over to the passenger side door of a Chrysler Lebaron; Don was leaning in the driver's side, placing some human skin in an evidence bag. He looked up at Bob and said, 'You smell that?'

Bob nodded. 'Yeah, pretty nasty, gonna get a lot worse once the sun comes out from behind those clouds.'

'No.' He shook his head, 'that other smell.'

Bob gave him a perplexed look. 'What are you talking about?'

Don broke into a huge smile. 'It still has that new car smell.' He laughed and ducked back inside to continue his evidence collecting.

Bob shook his head, he couldn't help but laugh. He knelt down and examined the inside of a door. 'There's something strange about all this,' Bob voiced.

'Yeah, no shit?' Don replied.

'No, no, no. You don't get what I'm saying. Look here, notice there's no blood run or drag spatter? No signs of a struggle? It's as if it didn't happen here, it almost looks… staged, doesn't it?'

Don looked around and clearly came to the same conclusion. 'Holy shit, Sarge, you're right.'

Bob continued, 'The blood that's here and over here - well everywhere – it all seems perfectly proportioned; it kinda looks like it was placed. Almost like everything was perfectly positioned to make it look, well – horrific.'

'Well they did a damn good job if you asked me,' Don said matter-of-factly. His phone chimed and he pulled it out. 'And Irene from the lab just confirmed the blood is definitely human. She says she'll have an ID on the garbage bag of hands I gave her within the hour.'

Both heard a loud thump on the roof of the car and looked at each other startled. They exited the car in time to watch a female head roll off the roof and down the windshield. It came to rest on the front hood wiper blades. It was staring right at them. Bob noticed its freshness.

No decomposition he thought.

It still had normal skin colour, the eyes were bright blue and moist. If it wasn't for the whole missing her body thing, she looked alive.

'This is pretty fucked up, huh, Bob?' Don began to show his nervousness, his voice cracked a little.

Bob nodded. '*Really* fucked up.'

They both looked up. A photo tech, hoisted on a rope high above them, was photographing a torso in a skirt. Seeing the two detectives scowling faces, he quickly yelled, 'Sorry guys.'

Bob Snook stood by the coffee counter of Hindis Quiki Mart with Don Foito, when a rather large woman in pink stretch pants walked in. She looked sullen and miserable until she made eye contact with Foito. They exchanged smiles and Bob squirmed.

'Sorry, man, just don't know how you can do it.'

'C'mon Sarge, don't knock it until you've *knocked it*.' Bob followed Foito's eyes as they fixed in on the very pronounced crack of her ass.

'Mmm, mmm,' he hummed.

Bob rolled his eyes.

Foito continued, 'They are so appreciative afterwards too, ya know. Matter of fact, if they're real good, I bring em right here, let them have their pick of anything on the top shelf.'

Snook couldn't help but look up. He shook his head sadly at the selection of hostess crumb cakes. Don was about to impart more unwanted information about his fetish, when Bob was saved by his phone ringing.

'Snook. Hey Irene, talk to me. Really? That's…. Are you sure? Okay, thanks Irene.'

Bob clipped his phone back onto his belt. He was trying to make sense of the information he just got, but he simply couldn't. He was more confused now than ever.

'What's up, Sarge?'

He turned to Foito. 'We got a match on that bag of hands.'

'Good.' Foito took his eyes off the pink love goddess

'No, it is not good, Don, nothing about this situation is good. As best as Irene can tell, as not everyone is in the system, most of the ones she could identify are from people who died more than fifty years ago.' Bob Snook sipped his coffee in disbelief.

The River of Puss, Hell

'Stop asking me that, I don't know why.' Miles sighed dramatically. 'And why does it fucking matter?'

Ethan turned. 'It matters, Miles. Listen to me.' He crouched down. 'I'm not meant to be here, I understand now. You died in a car accident. I didn't die. I was dragged here, still alive.'

'So what? You're still in Hell, what does it matter if you're dead or alive? There's no escape for anyone.'

'Well, possibly not for anyone who *died* in the real world, but what if you hadn't died?'

Miles shrugged. 'How do you know this isn't some fucked up game?'

'I don't.' Ethan rubbed his chin. 'But I'm willing to put my theory to the test.'

'How?'

'Simple.' Ethan, head held high, as naked as the day he was born, walked with purpose off the rock, right into the river of puss. As his feet made contact the river parted for him. He stepped down onto an exposed rock and the river continued to retreat. He turned to Miles. 'Are you coming?' Miles looked in shock at what was happening, he quickly getting to his feet.

'How are you doing that?'

'I'm not meant to be here, Miles. I was being tested by God for some reason. Maybe he made a deal with Lucifer, the same kind of deal he made with Job. I assumed because he took me, I'd failed the test – But now I'm beginning to suspect the test is still running. We must have faith, Miles.'

'I don't have any faith, Ethan, not anymore. I'm not a good person.' He lowered his gaze.

'But are you an evil person?'

Miles shrugged. 'I'm in Hell, ain't I. I suppose I must be.'

Ethan held out a hand. 'Follow me, Miles. I don't think you're meant to be here either. I think you were caught in the wake of your friend, Marco. Let us escape this place together.'

Miles shook his head. 'What happens to me if we leave? I'm already dead. I ain't gonna be some zombie eating brains.'

'Miles, you watch far too much television. Besides, you want to be here, in this place, for eternity, or out there in the real world?'

'Of course I want to be in the real world.'

'Even if that means eating brains?' He laughed.

'Funny.'

'Then grow some balls, man.' He held out his hand, 'follow me.'

Miles shakily stepped off the rock and down to where the river had parted. He expected to be dragged in as he took Ethan's hand. He expected demonic creatures to rise up and pull him under, to repeat the same nightmares over and over. He took pigeon steps, looking as best he could with only one eye, left and right. If his heart was beating, it would have been heard from miles away. Ethan held his hand tightly.

'We're good, Miles, we can escape this place, get back to the real world, c'mon.' They continued to step down, and the river roared away from them. They walked along a stony path downwards, for many hours. Eventually they found the river's bed. As they walked along the expanding path, Miles looked up at the walls on each side of them, made by the river, flowing hundreds of feet high above them. As they walked along the bed, the river parted ahead of them. To Miles' horror, he saw that the way back was gone.

'Ain't this like Jesus parting the Dead Sea?'

'Moses, Miles, he parted the *Red Sea.*'

'Oh.'

Ethan smiled at him. 'Faith, Miles. We'll make it.' And together they walked. Two men. Naked. Hand in hand along the bed of the river of puss.

After many hours or possibly days, they came to a steep impenetrable stone wall. There was no possible way of navigating it and Miles began, again, to panic. Ethan let go of his hand and looked up at it. He murmured a prayer. A shaft of light burst through the fire in the sky; it illuminated a dark recess that hadn't been there before.

'This way, Miles.' Ethan grabbed the frightened man's hand and dragged him into the cave.

Somewhere deep in the Republic of Sudan

Never did learn how to swim. O'Conner thought as the helicopter touched down on the *Beaconhurst* Cruise Ship. *Doesn't matter here though.*

Mark O'Conner was met by a German United Nations officer whose nametag read Klaus Hoffenberg. O'Conner did his best to hide his surprise but Klaus caught the look and knew exactly what he was thinking. In his best Jewish accent Klaus said: 'My grandfather wanted to be the first to break the social barriers after the War, and my grandmother, well, she simply fucked her way out of the ovens.' He laughed and stepped forward, shaking O'Conner's hand. 'Welcome to Sudan, Special Agent O'Conner. We've been expecting you.'

Mark O'Conner was taken back, and impressed with Klaus's intuitiveness.

Klaus became very serious. 'Are you ready for this, Special Agent?'

'Call me Mark and nothing surprises me anymore, Klaus.'

They passed by numerous investigators, photo tech and military police, all going about their business. Mark stopped and looked around at the barring sea - of desert. There was nothing but sand as far as the eye could see. He shook his head in disbelief as he entered through one of the ships port doors. Klaus spoke as they walked:

'At 08:52hrs GMT, intelligence picked up chatter from the Libyan Air Force.' Mark raised an eyebrow and Klaus momentarily chuckled. He continued. 'Okay, so one of their four pilots had drawn the short straw and was flying one of only two working F-10's over the south province of Sudan. We thought he must have been hitting the hookah when he reported seeing the seven-story, two-thousand passenger ship sitting smack in the middle of the desert. But here we are.'

'Let me guess.' O'Conner interrupted. 'You have a ship full of body parts, no ID on any of them, and everything looks staged?'

Klaus looked surprised and impressed. 'You guessed right, Special Agent, but with one addition.'

Klaus opened both doors leading to the grand solarium located in the centre of the ship. O'Conner walked in and was awed by the sight. They stood on the upper level, a grandioso of fine ship making workmanship, looking down at all seven stories. Each level open to a view of fine woods, brass, gold, silver, and mahoganies, huge glittering chandeliers, and hanging light fixtures - all covered in blood, flesh, guts and shit.' O'Conner was not at all taken back with the pandemonium and body parts. He's seen more corpse and parts in the past three days then a laundry guy at Auschwitz. But he was very curious of the blood patterns on the walls and floors.

This is *new,* he thought.

Klaus answered his unspoken question. 'We think they are tentacle marks.'

Mark looked at him in disbelief. 'In the desert? Inside a ship? With no damage to the hull?'

Klaus nodded and shrugged. 'Our best biologists worked hard to verify the markings and they came back with the conclusion, as farfetched as it may sound to us, that they think it *might* be tentacles – octopus to be specific. To be precise, to make marks like that, it would have to be around a one-thousand ton octopus.' He shrugged again. 'We sent tissue samples to every lab, they come back, well, they come back nothing.'

'Nothing?'

'That's right, Special Agent, nothing. They simply don't match anything.'

'That's impossible, Klaus, they have to match something. Tell your guy to send the tissue samples to Quantico. Nothing personal, but let's get a second opinion.'

'Of course.'

Mark's phone rang and he grabbed it off his belt. 'O'Conner.'

He listened for a few seconds and replied, 'I'm on my way. Yeah, some interesting developments, we now have sea monsters, apparently. Yeah, I'm being serious. Well no, nothing else new. Same shit, different location. I'll be there in about ten hours give or take; I'm on my way to the plan now.' He hung up, turned to Klaus and reached out and shook his hand.

'Something I should know about, Special Agent?'

Mark called out over his shoulder, 'I think I found your missing ocean, and it just covered the entire state of Colorado.'

Somewhere deep in the bowels of Hell

'How do you know where you're going?'

'Because I have...'

'...faith, sorry, I know.'

Ethan smiled at him. 'You're still unsure, aren't you?'

'I don't trust my eyes.' He sighed. 'Eye.'

'I understand that, Miles, you have no reason to trust me. We've only just met. But listen to me, for a moment. I can't explain everything to you. I don't know what is going to happen to either of us, if we'll even get out of here.' He chuckled as he said it, 'alive. But if you don't try, if you allow yourself to wallow in self-pity, you'll never get anywhere, always be stuck in this nightmare.'

'It's hard to take you seriously, Ethan, when you're naked.' Miles smiled at him.

'That's the spirit, c'mon, we can get out of here Miles, you and me. We will defeat him and prove our faith in God is not misplaced.'

'Ethan, I don't believe in God.' He looked miserable.

'That's okay, Miles. He believes in you.' They continued on through winding passageways, through cracks in rocks and when they found themselves lost, a mysterious light would always appear to guide them on.

Up and up they walked for hours and hours. They did not grow weary and they chatted along the way. Miles was more at ease now than ever before, mostly because they hadn't seen anything horrific since entering the cave and Ethan was so positive they would escape, his infectious enthusiasm made it possible for him to really, truthfully believe it. The first sparks of hope energised him. After many more hours, they finally come to a door.

Without pause, Ethan grabbed for the handle and twisted it. The door opened quietly enough and he grinned, grabbed Miles quickly by the hand, and pulled him through.

Colorado

As the helicopter landed on top of the Rocky Mountains, O'Conner witnessed in disbelief hundreds of soldiers all in combat stance hysterically shooting in every direction at bears, mountain lions, bobcats, wolves, and charging elks. They were all fighting for the extremely limited space – and the soldiers were losing ground.

As far as his eyes could see, was the sea.

The pilot looked uncertainly at O'Conner, who gave him *a thumb* up to get the hell out of there. He had seen all he needed to. As they ascended and flew off, O'Conner looked on in horror. The soldiers were retreating, the animals sensing victory were charging forward. He observed a soldier trying to reload, but not quickly enough. He was quickly impaled by a charging elk antler and dragged forward by the animal's momentum. Another soldier, his ammo depleted, was overtaken and ripped to pieces by a pack of wolves. The scene played out over and over, hundreds of men, butchered and mutilated. Despite the piles of animal carcasses building around them, both sides were relentless in their pursuit of victory. A grizzly bear effortlessly swiped the head off the commanding officer – his body dropped and was dragged off by a lioness. Her cubs pulled out his intestines.

'Jesus Christ!' he voiced. O'Conner keyed the helmet microphone and ordered the pilot to connect him with the Washington Office. After several seconds of static, a voice broke through.

'O'Conner?' It was the SAIC who spoke. 'What's your status?'

'It's all under water, sir. I'm waiting for further instructions.'

There was a long static pause. The SAIC finally spoke, 'There aren't any, Mark. Go home to your family.'

There was another long paused. 'We just lost contact with Air Force One, and there's been some kind of attack on the White House. Mark, there's nothing left of it.'

O'Conner and the pilot exchanged looks as the communication burst into static and went dead.

The pilot blinked a couple of times before saying: 'Sir?'

Mark turned and looked ahead; he contemplated an answer for several seconds. Eventually he turned to the pilot. A look of resignation in his face.

'Just find some dry land… and a bar.'

O'Conner had never been a drinker. He'd prided himself that he'd never given in to that vice; he'd always managed to get through the worst of the job without resorting to alcohol to escape from it. That was then, he reflected; today he was content to stare deeply into the freshly poured shot of Scotch in front of him on the bar, whilst holding a tall glass of beer. He slowly reached for the shot and brought it up to his lips - and paused.

It was a moment of judgement.

A voice spoke from the other side of the bar. He looked up to see the bartender carefully cleaning a glass. 'Looks like you could use that.'

Mark looked back at the glass in his hand. It hovered at his lips, close enough now he could almost taste it. Eventually his choice was made. He downed it, winced with a bitter expression, and followed it up with a sip of beer.

The bartender immediately refilled the shot glass.

'This ones on me, buddy.'

Mark looked up at him and nodded in appreciation.

'What's your name?' Mark asked, throwing the fresh shot down his throat. Again the glass was refilled.

'It's Lou.'

Mark smiled. 'Lou?'

Lou laughed. 'Yeah I know, you could have guessed that one, huh?'

'So Lou, you ready for the end of the world?'

Mark took another sip of his beer.

Lou smiled. 'Oh no, my friend. Don't look at it as the end. Think of it as a new beginning.' He lifted the bottle, Mark nodded. 'Hit me.'

'Are you a religious man?' Lou asked.

Mark smiled. 'I used to be.'

Lou handed him four sugar cubes. Mark looked at them inquisitively. 'What are these for?'

'Well,' Lou said matter-of-factly. 'If it's the end of the world, as you say, you're gonna need these for the four horses.'

Mark laughed and downed the second shot.

He looked up at the television, the news was on, but there was no sound. The picture showed the White House, levelled and burning.

'Lou, can you turn that up?'

Lou handed him the remote.

'Feel free to change the channel to something less depressing.' He filled Mark's shot glass once again.

Mark changed the channel several times. Each time it was the same breaking news. *One more channel and if it's still the news he was simply going to shut it off.*

The television finally showed a station that wasn't displaying world news. An interviewer, standing on a red carpet spoke: *'And in television news, upcoming writer and director, Will Sampago has just finished up the first of three episodes of what is believed to be a world classic series of action, horror, and thriller adventures entitled* Revolting Tales, *expected to be out this spring. We're live with studio boss, Maurice Zinkiewicz as Will is currently working hard on the series and unable to be here today. Thank you for joining us, Michael.'*

'It's a pleasure to be here, Anne.'

'Can you tell us a little more about the series, what it's about?'

'Of course. It's essentially a selection of macabre tales, depicting the demise of some of the most horrendously vile people on the planet. As each episode goes by, we'll start to see more and more people find retribution at the hands of some of the worst kinds of demons. It's grisly stuff!'

'Interesting. You say demons, is this going to be just another zombie flick?'

'No, no, not at all. You can't get away from zombies these days, Anne, but they do sell! No, we have an amazing script and I assure you and the people at home, you'll be on the edge of your seats, and behind them at times, as we delve into some pretty difficult and truly inspiring ethical situations. I can't promise you won't see a zombie or two, but you won't see them like you have before, that I will promise.'

'Thank you, Maurice. Well, we have an exclusive clip now for you. I should warn you, it's pretty nasty, so if you don't like blood and gore, look away now.'

The picture shifted to a shot of a car dealership, and Mark watched in growing horror as the show depicted a truly horrendous scene of violence. Cars piled up high, blood and guts and shit everywhere. Dismembered bodies, heads, and feet; it was awful and graphic but that wasn't the worst of it, Mark realised with he'd seen this all before… he continued to watch out of curiosity and disbelief.

What he was watching was impossible.

'It can't be.'

Lou spoke. 'Looks like you've seen a ghost my friend.'

Mark got up and pulled out his billfold. 'Maybe Lou….just maybe.'

He fumbled for some cash but couldn't find any.

Lou shook his head. 'No, no, no, my friend, it's on the house.'
Mark smiled in relief. 'I owe you one, Lou.'
'And I'll hold you to that, Mark.' Lou replied with a wink.

ME Office, Madison - Connecticut

Bob Snook looked in disgust as Foito took a long and deep sniff from a shoeless foot. 'Look, no smell, Sarge.'

It was a very busy autopsy room. Everyone was active. Every stainless steel table was full of sorted piles of body parts. There were mounds of them in every corner of the room.

Foito was right there were no smells of decaying flesh, sweaty feet, or coagulation blood. The state examiner held up what appeared to be a stomach, moist, wet, dripping in blood. He sniffed it himself. He shook his head in disbelief.

Bob's phone rang.

'Snook,' he answered. 'Hey Mark, what's up?'

He listened for several seconds making several facial expressions of doubt.

'Okay, my friend, if you say so.' Snook hung up and looked at Foito.

'Come on. We're going to the movies.'

Newton Brown Television Studio

The helicopter landed in the parking lot of a local supermarket cordoned off by the local police. Bob Snook and Don Foito were waiting with the car as Mark O'Conner slipped out the door head down. He ran towards them.

'What's going on, Mark?'

'I'll explain in the car, let's go.'

Bob put the car in drive, grabbed the wheel. They sped off in the direction of the studio. It was only a block or two away. Mark quickly got them up to speed on what he'd seen of the disasters and incidents around the world, and what had brought him here.

'I don't know much. But I do know the studio making the TV show is responsible for everything. Somehow.'

Foito gave him a look. 'Really?' He turned to Snook. 'C'mon Sarge, he's lost it.'

Bob ignored him. 'You say you saw the scene we were at on one of these shows?'

'Identical, Bob. Right down to the stack of cars.'

'Makes some kind of perverse sense, I suppose, could be a coincidence as well, Mark.'

'Look, Bob, I don't understand it either, but I'm telling you we gotta stop them.'

'Stop them? How? Go in there and tell them to stop making a TV show, cos it's destroying the world? Be reasonable, Mark.'

Mark put his hand on the back of his neck. 'For god sake, Bob. Have you seen the news lately?'

Bob slammed on the brakes. He turned sharply. 'I don't have to be reasonable, Mark. I have no answer for anything that's going on in the world. But then again, I've never paid a lot of attention to anything outside of my own little bubble, and that has served me well all these years, so excuse me if I don't get all mopey over a few unexplained incidents, okay?'

Mark calmed himself. Don went to say something, but Bob caught the movement and slapped him in the face. 'Shut the fuck up, Foito.' Bob said.

'Jesus Chris, Sarge!' Don rubbed his cheekbone.

'Bob, let's just go there and take a look. If we don't find a set that looks identical to the car dealership you can cuff me and stick me in the psych ward, deal?'

Bob grunted and turned back to the wheel. He slipped the car into drive and caught Don's look as he sped on.

'What the fuck, Foito, I barely touched you.'

They drove up to the main gates and a security guard stepped out, he put his hand up for them to stop.

'Leave this to me,' Snook said.

The guard came up to the driver's side window and Bob opened it.

'How you doing? We got a call about some suspicious activity in the area,' he said as he pulled out his badge. 'Detectives Snook and Foito. We're just going to take a look around, make sure everything is clean, so be a good boy and open the gates up.'

'Sorry, sir. This is private property. You can't come in here without a warrant.'

'Like I said, we're here on a call. We can do this the easy way, or the hard way. It's your choice.'

The guard sneered. 'No warrant, no entry.'

Bob narrowed his eyes slightly. 'I know you.'

The guard shrugged slightly. 'What of it?'

'Marcik? Tommy Marcik right?'

He was suddenly less sure of himself.

'Well, well, well. Who the fuck knew? Tommy Marcik.'

'It doesn't make any difference.'

Snook stepped out of the car. 'The hell it doesn't. The case is still open, Marcik, we never closed it. Dirty fucking cops give us all a bad name.' He looked at him in disgust. Marcik met his glare, but elected to say nothing.

'Not so cock sure now, eh?'

'Just doin' my job.'

'Don't give me that crap. Get that fucking gate open, Marcik, or I'll make life so fucking awful...'

Tommy was already heading for his booth. 'Fine you can go in, but I'm making an official complaint.'

Snook stared at him a moment longer, then got back in the car.

'Fuck you very much,' he said, as they entered the grounds of the studio.

The guard went back to his hut and lifted the electronic barrier. The car pulled slowly up towards the first large building they could see.

The other side of the door

Ethan and Miles were standing in an empty alleyway. A neon sign, *Caesar's Palace*, flickered and flashed and was the only real source of illumination. They had emerged from behind an old dumpster; Ethan recognised it as the one he was pulled into by Lou. He wasn't sure where they should go next, but the cold night, which made him shiver, felt good.

It felt normal. It felt real.

'I think we're out, Miles.'

'Really?'

'Yeah, don't you feel it? The coldness, the smell of the air, we're home, and we really need to find some clothes.'

'I don't feel anything,' Miles said.

Ethan noted he still wasn't breathing. 'I forgot, you're dead.'

'Dead? What am I? A zombie?'

'I don't know, Miles. Let's head over this way, I think I can see a light. It might be a house. Maybe we can get some help.' Ethan grabbed Miles by the elbow who reluctantly started to jog with him towards the light he couldn't see. They pushed through a heavily overgrown set of bushes, which seemed to grab at them as they did so. Ethan resolutely pushed on, all the time encouraging Miles. Eventually they emerged in the grounds of an old mansion. There was a light at the uppermost window and Ethan and Miles ran to the door. They banged hard, but no one came. Ethan looked around and found a pull chain, as old fashioned as the house, but he pulled it none-the-less. From deep inside the house, they heard a bell clang.

Still no one came.

'Looks empty, Ethan.'

He nodded. 'Yes, but there might be some clothes inside, a telephone maybe. I don't know, let's try and find a way in.'

Miles took a step back and was about to say something, when a little girl appeared beside him from nowhere, and carefully slipped her hand into his.

Newton Brown Television Studio

'This is fucking bullshit,' Foito said as the three of them walked around the car dealership set, an exact replica of the real one they'd been investigation.

'This is bullshit,' he said again. 'I'm telling you, Sarge, this is…'

'If you say bullshit one more time, Foito, I swear I will eat you, and shit you out on your mother's lawn.'

Don flinched. 'Sorry, Sarge.'

Mark took his glasses off. 'Bob, you believe me now?'

Snook surveyed the area nodding. 'Yeah, Mark. Yeah, I believe you. But I don't know what to think about all this.'

'Let's find the studio they're filming in, we've got to stop them, Bob.'

'Yeah, Mark. Let's do that.'

After a minute or two, they found a group of cars and people all milling about around a large hangar. The three of them walked up to a truck a group of kids were carefully unloading. They flashed their badges.

'Where's the boss?' Mark asked gruffly.

'You mean Will?' one of the boys asked, still unloading the heavy bags.

'Well if he's the guy running the show, then yeah, I mean Will.'

'He's up in building Four-A , sir. They're shooting this really cool scene right now.'

Bob stepped forward. 'What kind of scene?'

'Oh I don't know much, but it's like a big bomb that goes off somewhere, like a nuclear bomb or something.'

They all shouted at the same time.

'Show us the building!'

The Empty House

Miles looked down at the black haired little girl as she gripped his hand tightly.

'Erm… Ethan?'

Ethan turned and stopped dead. There was a little girl holding Miles' hand and she looked dead. He stepped forward and she covered her eyes with her right hand.

'Oh! You're both naked! I'm not allowed to look.' She giggled.

Miles didn't know what to do and as Ethan had a look of horror on his face, he wasn't feeling too comfortable. Ethan pushed through his initial fear, mainly because he needed to show Miles everything was okay. He stepped forward and dropped to one knee.

'What's your name, little girl?'

'Matilda,' she said sucking on her right thumb. 'What's yours?'

'Ethan.'

'I like your friend, can I keep him?' she looked up at Miles and smiled as her dead eyes met his. She released his hand and then put her arms up in a way a child does when they want to be carried. Miles didn't want to touch her, but he also didn't want to upset her either. Ethan nodded at him, so he reached down and lifted her up. She clung to his neck.

'What are you doing out so late at night?' Miles asked her.

She giggled in response.

'You're funny, Miles.'

He suddenly became fearful again. 'How do you know my name?'

She giggled.

'Take me over there.' She pointed to an old willow tree.

Miles felt an odd compunction to obey. Ethan felt the evil around him and tried to stop him. As he got close, Matilda turned and uttered a feral shriek at him, her face became demonic and her sharp little teeth gnashed at him. Miles continued to move toward the old tree as if under some spell. He set her down and she skipped away. Ethan cautiously joined him.

'Miles, we need to leave this place, there is great evil here.'

Before either of them could act, a branch swept down and threw them like a rag doll into its trunk. Instantly branches came to life, grabbing both the naked Priest and Miles, lifting them by their ankles high into the air. They both screamed in terror. The tree came fully alive, its wide red melon sized eyes staring at them both. It lifted each man towards a gapping, twisted mouth, full of sharp wooden teeth.

Ethan watched helplessly as Miles and he were slowly lowered towards slavering jaws...

Newton Brown Television Studio

Mark, Bob and Don pushed their way into the studio and each was shouting as they finally made it up to the room that Will was working in. There was so much confusion, as the two cops and one FBI agent were waving guns and badges around.

'You've got to stop!' they were shouting together.

People stopped what they were doing.

Actors stopped rehearsing.

Production stopped.

Will Sampago turned to the "fx" guys in the booth and said, 'Jesus fucking Christ, I'll go see what these idiots want. Time is money, boys. Just get on with things up here, and drop that fucking bomb!'

The end...?

We see the camera zoom slowly into a table.
We hear the sounds of people yelling and shouting coming from close by.

The desk is heavily laden with papers and books, piles upon piles of notes and other miscellaneous items, but the camera picks out a lone Bobblehead Jesus.

It zooms in closer and closer.

The head now fills the screen entirely. The camera holds on the image, and just before the screen goes black, it bobbles.

Three words appear in the centre.

...to be continued...

About Todd A Curry

Todd is one of seven siblings from what he describes as: "A pleasantly dysfunctional family."

Todd's exuberant youth left him with two clear career choices, when he graduated high school in 1976. Jail or Service. He decided on the latter and joined the Army. Ironically, Todd became a Military Policeman and subsequently attended the Academy for Specialized Military Police Investigators. He excelled and moved quickly up to the rank of sergeant, awarded an assignment in United States Criminal Investigation's Division, a covert narcotics investigation team, both here and abroad. He left the service in 1983 and worked briefly as a correctional officer. Fearing confinement and believing his position was one step above an inmate, he left to become a police officer. He worked as Patrol Dog handler for 6 years, followed by a 3 year tour with the State Anti-terrorism Task Force (SATTF) as a field investigator and certified criminal analyst. He returned to his Police Department and commanded the Criminal Investigations Division for the remainder of his career.

Detective Sergeant Curry is the recipient of two medals of bravery, and many others he won't talk about, from a career that spanned thirty years.

"I've seen things I wish I hadn't and I've experienced things that few have. I found it oddly satisfying and more comforting running toward danger and basking in its horrifying aura, than the uncomfortable feeling I got sending someone else to do it."

"Not surprisingly my first book is a series of short horror stories….go figure."

About Christopher D. Abbott

Christopher D. Abbott has a background in human behavioural studies. Having worked in IT, communications, safety and health, and sales, he has gained a good understanding about people and their behaviours. This has led to his interest in psychology. For many years, he has been an avid reader of crime fiction. Christopher has taken creative writing courses and from this, his ambition was always to publish a character driven crime story, in the style of the great Agatha Christie. Christopher loves quirky characters, such as Rodney David Wingfield's Inspector "Jack" Frost, along with Agatha Christie's Poirot, and Sir Arthur Conan Doyle's Sherlock Holmes. The Idea of Doctor Pieter Straay, his Dutch Criminal Psychologist, came about by integrating the qualities he admired best in the three previous characters.

Christopher grew up in England and moved to the United States in 2010. He currently resides in Connecticut. He loves to write and has two published stories. His debut novel, *Sir Laurence Dies*, and a short story entitled *The House*, in a collection of short horror stories: *All That Remains*. He enjoys playing music, which has been as much of a passion for him as writing is. He also enjoys cooking and is currently working on his next Doctor Straay novel and the autobiography of Todd A. Curry.

24024833R00110

Made in the USA
Charleston, SC
11 November 2013